"Trust me—you're better off without him."

A curious mixture of simmering fury—not directed at her, but on her behalf—and compassion filled Jonas's dark eyes. AnnaBeth gaped at him. She reminded herself to breathe.

No one had ever defended her supposedly injured honor so vigorously before.

She didn't know what to say. And for once, surprising herself, she said nothing.

"Storm's likely to last all night. We could be snowed in a few days." A muscle jumped in his jaw.

He said he knew—*as in understood firsthand?*—that she was better off without her erstwhile groom. In the past, had something as equally humiliating and hurtful happened to him, too?

Jonas squared his broad shoulders. "Stay here as long as you like, AnnaBeth. You've found a refuge from the storm here with us."

Her heart gave a funny quiver. Her eyes locked with his. She became lost in his melted-chocolate eyes.

Lisa Carter and her family make their home in North Carolina. In addition to her Love Inspired novels, she writes romantic suspense for Abingdon Press. When she isn't writing, Lisa enjoys traveling to romantic locales, teaching writing workshops and researching her next exotic adventure. She has strong opinions on barbecue and ACC basketball. She loves to hear from readers. Connect with Lisa at lisacarterauthor.com.

Books by Lisa Carter

Love Inspired

Visit the Author Profile page at Harlequin.com.

Stranded
for the Holidays

Lisa Carter

Recycling programs for this product may not exist in your area.

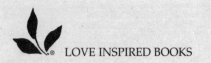

LOVE INSPIRED BOOKS

ISBN-13: 978-1-335-53962-5

Stranded for the Holidays

Copyright © 2019 by Lisa Carter

www.Harlequin.com

Printed in U.S.A.

Surely he shall not be moved for ever: the righteous shall be in everlasting remembrance. He shall not be afraid of evil tidings: his heart is fixed, trusting in the Lord.
—*Psalm* 112:6–7

In thanksgiving to the great and holy Immanuel—God with us. He came down from Heaven to dwell among us so that we might behold His glory, the glory of the Son of God. It is through Him we become the children of God and have eternal life.

Chapter One

Grinning, Jonas Stone snapped a quick photo of his son. In a pint-size Stetson and cowboy boots, four-year-old Hunter looked adorable sitting in Santa's lap.

From the mounted loudspeakers at the edge of the town square, strains of "Winter Wonderland" provided a festive note. Friends called out greetings to each other.

Pretty much the entire population of Truelove, North Carolina had turned out for the annual Christmas parade. And also for the free hot chocolate, courtesy of the Mason Jar, the local diner on the other side of the green.

Nursing a cold, Jonas's mother had remained at the ranch, opting to skip the parade and the visit with Santa. Per tradition, the Truelove Christmas parade always landed on the Saturday after Thanksgiving.

But it seemed to Jonas that Christmas came earlier every year. At least, the trappings of Christmas. If it wasn't for his son, he'd just as soon bypass the holidays.

Or maybe he was getting old. Old, alone and—according to his also widowed mother—dangerously close to being forever set in his grumpy ways.

Enthroned in the gazebo, Santa—aka Truelove's mayor—patted Hunter's jean-clad knee. "Have you been a good boy this year?"

"I think so, Santa." Hunter's dark brown eyes swung to Jonas. "And a weally good cowboy, too. Wight, Dad?"

His son's breath fogged in the crisp, mountain air. The cold front and plummeting temperature had necessitated pulling out their winter coats before they'd left the ranch this morning.

Jonas smiled at his little cowboy. "A very good cowboy."

"Mrs. Santa will be so pleased." Mayor Watson's pale blue eyes twinkled. "And what is it you'd like Santa to bring you this Christmas, my boy?"

Hunter's eyebrows drew together like twin caterpillars. "It's some-ding I weally, weally want, Santa." Cupping his mitten, he whispered in Santa's ear.

Jonas scanned the Blue Ridge vista surrounding the small Appalachian community. Low, thin clouds enveloped the mountains. The chill in the air hinted of coming snow.

And if it wasn't already snowing on the mountain at FieldStone Ranch, it soon would be. They'd need to get on the road soon.

"You're sure that's what you want for Christmas, Hunter?"

At the note of concern in Mayor Watson's voice, Jonas turned from his contemplation of the dreary skyline. Hunter's head bobbed. "I'm sure."

With the freezing temperature, Mayor Watson's rather bulbous nose had turned an appropriate cherry-red. "Not a new rope? Or a saddle? Or—"

"Dat's the only ding I want for Chwismas, Santa." Hunter's face turned unusually solemn.

Watson tugged at his snow-white beard. "That sort of gift is kinda hard to come by." His eyes darted to Jonas. "And best given by your father."

"But Dad's gonna need your help, Santa." Hunter crossed his arms over his skinny chest. "Gwam-ma says, God's help, too."

Jonas raised an eyebrow. "Wow, that must be some gift."

Watson chuckled nervously. "Thank you for coming to see me today, Hunter." He eased the little boy off his lap. "I hope you have a merry Christmas. Make sure you get a candy cane from my helper."

He steered Hunter toward the steps, where the grandmotherly ErmaJean Hicks waited. With her silvery hair tucked inside a green felt hat, she resembled a jolly, if somewhat plump, elderly elf.

Watson caught Jonas's coat sleeve. "Uh, Stone. I feel I ought to warn you."

He frowned. "Warn me? About what?"

"I'd hate for Hunter to be disappointed." The mayor cut his eyes to where Hunter waited at the bottom of the steps, happily licking the red stripe off the peppermint cane. "Telling a Christmas wish isn't the same as blabbing a birthday wish…"

"Hunter's a great kid," Jonas agreed. "If he only wants one thing for Christmas, I'll do my best to make sure he gets it."

The mayor cleared his throat. "Fact is, Jonas, the only thing Hunter wants for Christmas this year is a mommy."

Jonas stared at him. "A what?"

"You heard me." Watson winced. "I wish you well with that. Next?"

He moved aside as Hunter's best friend, little Maisie McAbee, scrambled onto Santa's lap, clutching a list in her small hand.

What had just happened?

"Here." Smirking, ErmaJean thrust a candy cane at Jonas. "Out of the mouths of babes."

Stifling a groan, he scanned the crowd milling around the square for the rest of the Double Name

Club—GeorgeAnne Allen and his great-aunt, Ida-Lee Moore. The trio were notoriously known as the Truelove Matchmakers, and where there was one, the others weren't usually too far behind.

The three old ladies were infamous for poking their noses where they didn't belong. They took the town motto—Truelove, Where True Love Awaits—a little too seriously.

Ethan Green—ErmaJean's grandson—and his wife, Amber, had been the matchmakers' most recent matrimonial success story.

But after Jonas's wife, Kasey, walked out on them, he had decided women were trouble he didn't need. He'd take his life on the ranch with Hunter any day over some high-maintenance, commitment-phobic woman. He didn't need that kind of heartache. Once burned, twice shy.

Clamping his Stetson onto his head, he shouldered past the older lady. "Excuse me, Miss Erma-Jean."

Married, divorced or spinster, the "Miss" was an honorary title of respect bestowed on any Southern lady who was your elder. No matter if the woman was elderly or not.

Lines fanned from the corners of ErmaJean's glacier-blue eyes. "You're on my radar now, Jonas Stone." She wagged a bony finger. "We wouldn't want to disappoint a child at Christmas, would we?"

Grunting, he took hold of his son. "On the way home, we need to have a talk, Hunter."

Shaken by the heartbreaking scene she'd stumbled upon, AnnaBeth Cummings ran toward the bridal dressing room. Gut clenching, she left her engagement ring beside her bouquet and quickly scribbled a note.

Please don't try to find me, Scott. Be happy, MaryDru. I'll be in touch. I need a little breathing room. All my love, AnnaBeth

Strains of organ music filtered from the sanctuary where family and friends awaited a Saturday-morning wedding that was never going to happen. The wedding her stepmother, Victoria, liked to call The Social Event of the Season.

AnnaBeth's heart raced. She had to hurry before it was too late. Before her father and Scott stopped her.

Or worse, Victoria, who was a force of nature. As in a hurricane. Tornado. Tidal wave. Firestorm.

She must make her getaway before Victoria could strong-arm her and Scott into doing something they'd regret.

AnnaBeth had no idea where she should go or what she should do with The Rest of Her Life. Yet a strange certainty that she was doing the right thing began to build inside her. And a budding excitement.

Grabbing her coat and her suitcase—she was glad it hadn't already been transferred to the limo—she ran for the parking lot. She ran for her life. She ran to find her life.

Leaf-barren trees lifted forlorn branches to the desolate, late November sky. Behind the wheel of her car, she turned off her cell phone and glanced in the rearview mirror. With a pained expression, she adjusted the ridiculously large, ivory satin bow affixed to the Juliet cap on her head a smidgeon. It didn't help.

"Sweet potatoes," she muttered.

But after such a dire beginning, the day could only get better from here. *Right?*

Snowflakes began to fall from the leaden sky. Headed west on Interstate 40, she drove for hours. Plenty of time to reflect on where everything had gone so catastrophically off-course.

Awaiting her father's arrival to escort her down the aisle, she'd been stricken with anxiety over her upcoming nuptials. So she'd decided to break tradition and see Scott one more time before the ceremony.

And discovered more than she'd ever bargained for when she found her two most favorite people in the world—Scott and her younger half sister, MaryDru—in each other's arms, saying an agonizing goodbye. She'd slipped away before either of them spotted her.

Images from the last few months filtered through her mind. Like suddenly coming upon her sister and Scott. The stammers. MaryDru's blushes. One or both of them always making an excuse for not being together in the same room.

How had everything gone so terribly wrong? How could she have not seen the love blossoming between her sister and Scott?

From the beginning, she'd had doubts about marrying Scott. But probably a thousand times since his proposal, she'd reassured herself that what she was feeling was nothing more than prewedding jitters.

So what if in their eight-month engagement he'd kissed her a total of once? So what if that one time had been akin to kissing a cousin? So what if there'd been no fireworks?

Not only had she not experienced lightning, but she'd also felt nothing.

She'd chalked it up to unrealistic expectations. She told herself they shared something far more solid than sparks—friendship. Their fathers were business associates and golf buddies. She and Scott had known one another forever.

"Love will grow," she whispered repeatedly. But it hadn't.

Now it wasn't so much sorrow she felt as giddy

relief. She didn't love Scott, and he didn't love her. She refused to stand in the way of MaryDru's happiness.

AnnaBeth's stomach growled. Perhaps it was time to refuel, and not just the gas tank. Last night at the rehearsal dinner, she hadn't eaten more than a bite. And in increasing dread of having to put on The Dress, she hadn't eaten much of anything for the past month.

She shivered. The higher the elevation, the colder it became. AnnaBeth turned the heat in the car on full-blast.

The slim-fitting mermaid wedding dress wasn't something she would've chosen for herself. Her hips weren't exactly her best feature, but Victoria had been insistent. Of course, the wedding dress would've been perfect for MaryDru.

After driving past a sign indicating a town called Truelove was ten miles ahead, she exited the highway and veered onto a secondary road. The irony of the town's name didn't escape her. Maybe when she stopped for gas, she'd meet the man of her dreams.

Hey, it wasn't impossible. Although, improbable. Yet stranger things had happened.

Right. She grimaced. *Keep telling yourself that, AnnaBeth.*

Had she learned nothing from her wedding

fiasco? Life didn't work like that. At least, not for her.

Snow began falling harder and faster, and dusted the winding double yellow line on the pavement. Shouldn't she have arrived in True-love already? She scanned the surrounding terrain, anxious for signs of civilization.

Behind her, the road had been swallowed by swirling snow. And just when she believed the situation couldn't get any worse, the car sputtered.

"No!" She strangled the wheel. "Don't quit on me now…"

But with a final convulsive jerk, the car shuddered to a stop. The engine died. This couldn't be happening. Not after everything else that had gone wrong today.

Don't panic. Try the ignition again. Please, please, please…

But nothing. Relinquishing her death grip on the wheel, she fell against the seat. Her heart pounded. What now?

Already the cold began to seep into the car. Snatching her phone off the console, she turned it on. No bars.

The deepening, storm-induced twilight would soon extinguish any last remnants of light from the sky. There was nothing to do but head on foot for the nearest shelter. Somewhere she'd taken a wrong turn. By now, she should've been in Truelove.

Story of her life. *Wrong turn, true love MIA... Film at eleven.*

AnnaBeth slipped her arms inside her wool coat, then grabbed her beaded clutch. She staggered out of the car and the wind almost knocked her down.

Having traveled about nine miles since leaving the interstate, if she followed the road, surely she'd encounter Truelove sooner rather than later.

In the blinding snow, she had difficulty establishing where the pavement began and ended. Yet sound traveled far over the snow-packed landscape, and after taking only a couple of tottering steps, she detected the sound of an engine in the distance.

Breathing a sigh of relief, she lifted her hand to flag her rescuer.

The snowstorm was turning out to be much worse than forecasters predicted. Driving conditions had grown increasingly hazardous the farther the truck climbed the mountain outside town.

Jonas would be relieved to reach the welcoming sanctuary of the ranch. As for the continuing conversation regarding a certain Christmas wish...

"Mommies don't just appear with a big wrapped bow under the tree on Christmas morning." He angled toward his son, strapped into a booster seat. "It doesn't work that way."

Hunter jabbed his thumb at the windshield. "Den what about her?"

A woman lurched onto the road in front of the pickup. For a split second, he wondered if he'd imagined her. Caught like a doe in the headlights, her eyes grew round with shock as she froze in the middle of the road.

He knew better, but he couldn't stop his knee-jerk reaction. Flinging one arm across his son, he slammed on the brakes. The tires hit a patch of ice and the vehicle fishtailed.

"Watch out, Dad," Hunter yelled.

But the pickup continued to slide forward. He fought the wheel, pumping the brakes to stop the truck's momentum.

God, please, help... Don't let me run her over.

With only inches to spare, he brought the truck to a grinding halt. His breathing ragged, his heart drummed in his chest. Through the back-and-forth motion of the windshield wipers, he stared at the woman with the slightly askew bow wrapped around her head.

"She's de one, Dad!" Bouncing in his seat, Hunter strained against the safety harness. "Dank You, God. Danks, Santa. She's de one I want for my mommy."

But as her eyes rolled into her head, the white-faced woman in the long, Christmas-green coat crumpled to the pavement.

He shut off the engine, and clambered out of the truck. Sick fear roiled his belly. He stared at the pale woman, lying motionless on the pavement. No blood. He could've sworn he hadn't hit her and yet…

Pressing two fingers to her neck, he checked for a pulse. Slightly elevated, but steady.

"Ma'am? Ma'am, can you hear me?"

Truck door slamming, Hunter joined him. They peered through the blowing snow at the woman on the ground.

Hunter's face scrunched. "Did you kill her, Dad?"

Adam's apple bobbing, he gulped. "I—I don't think so…"

"How come she doesn't wake up den?"

Good question. Grim scenarios of head and spinal injuries floated across his vision. But he couldn't leave her lying on the pavement. The freezing cold would send her into shock.

Hunter squatted beside the woman. "God sent us a pwetty one, didn't He, Dad?"

Jonas lifted his hat and resettled it on his head. "She's not…" But he could see where his son got the wrong idea about the woman.

A big bow on her head, frothy ruffles of fabric also peeped from underneath the hem of her bright green coat. She did look like a gift package. Wrapped especially for him.

Jonas frowned. Not him. Hunter. No… Not Hunter, either.

His son was right, though. She was a pretty woman. He couldn't tell the color of her eyes, but the reddish hue of her hair emphasized the alabaster fairness of her skin. She had a generous mouth—as if she did a lot of smiling.

Not that there was anything to smile about at the moment. Who was she? What was she doing on a deserted mountain road in a snowstorm?

Something catching his attention, Hunter wandered to the shoulder of the road. Returning, he handed a bead-covered purse to his father.

Jonas didn't like going through her private possessions, but if anything ever qualified as an emergency, he reckoned it was this. Lipstick. A brush. Breath mints. Keys…

His head came up. Squinting in the fading light, through the falling snow he discerned the dull glint of an automobile parked on the side of the road. She must have broken down or run out of gas.

A sports car. Something foreign. Something fast. And something that cost in the hundreds of thousands of dollars.

Not the usual vehicle found in the Blue Ridge.

Had she been on the parkway and gotten lost? He dug deeper into her purse.

A dead cell phone. A credit card. *Figured*. His efforts were rewarded when he came across a driver's license.

Hunkering near the woman, Hunter touched a tentative finger to the delicate skin on her hand. "She wooks wike a snow pwincess. Our snow pwincess."

"She's not our anything, Hunter. Her name is Anna... AnnaBeth..." He held the license to the beam of the headlights. "AnnaBeth Cummings."

Not from around here—her residence was listed as Charlotte. A flatlander—as if the fancy getup and expensive car hadn't already told him that.

"Maisie's got a book about a pwincess who fell a-sweep wike our snow pwincess." Elbows resting on his knees, Hunter cocked his head. His cowboy hat tilted. "The pwince has to kiss her to wake her up."

Jonas pinched the bridge of his nose. "We don't go around kissing people we don't know, son."

"But she's my mommy, Dad. It would be okay for me to kiss her, wouldn't it?"

And before Jonas could stop him, Hunter leaned over and kissed the woman's forehead.

She stirred.

"It's wowking, Dad." Hunter bolted to his feet. "I told you. Maisie was wight."

The woman's eyelids fluttered.

"Kiss her, Dad." Hunter tugged at his coat. "Help her wake up."

But it turned out the snow princess didn't need his help after all.

He found himself gazing into the loveliest, emerald-green eyes he'd ever seen. And something, not entirely unpleasant, shifted in his gut.

Snowflakes brushed AnnaBeth's cheeks. Her eyelids fluttered. She became aware of a biting cold. For inexplicable reasons, she found herself lying flat on her back in the road.

A cowboy stood over her. Two cowboys. Or maybe she was seeing double.

The smaller, duplicate cowboy leaned against the older one. Through her lashes, she took another quick, surreptitious look at the tall cowboy.

For a split second, she believed somehow she must've fallen backward to another place and time. Yet truck headlights glowed on the pavement, and she guessed she hadn't left present day. But, oh, how delicious this particular reality was turning out to be.

The older cowboy pushed the brim of his gray Stetson higher onto his forehead, revealing short-cropped blondish hair. His features were rugged. His jaw chiseled.

In short, he was every cowboy fantasy she'd

ever entertained, all rolled up in the man loom-
ing over her in the middle of the road.

A few years older than her, stark fear dotted his
chocolate-brown eyes.

If she hadn't already swooned, she would have
now. In the ordinary course of her life, she didn't
run across many men who looked like him.

He was so totally swoon-worthy. Maybe this
was a dream. A lovely, lovely dream from which
she hoped never to awaken.

AnnaBeth became aware that the little blond
boy—the mini-me cowboy—was speaking. Pat-
ting her hand, he smiled, his small teeth white,
even and perfect.

She thought he said, "You're going to be my
mommy."

But she must have misunderstood. And, anyway, the man—God's Cowboy Gift to Women—
said something she didn't catch in that delicious,
raspy voice of his.

She sighed, content to float forever in a cocoon
of bliss. "A lovely, lovely dream…"

"More like a nightmare," the cowboy growled.

Her eyes flew open. *Okeydokey.* He looked better than his manners. Trust AnnaBeth to find the
one grouchy cowboy on the planet.

Palms planted against the pavement, she pushed
to a sitting position. *Hello…*

As if someone had shaken a snow globe, the

truck, the boy, the man and her insides whirled. Her world spun.

The cowboy took hold of her elbow. "Not so fast, ma'am. Take it easy."

She put her hand to her head. Good to know he wasn't totally devoid of manners.

"Did you hit your head? Are you in pain?" He scanned her features. "Can you stand? Do you think anything's broken?"

Only my heart...

She gaped at him. Overwhelmed by the utter hunksomeness of him. *Stop gawking, AnnaBeth.*

Was she dead? If she was, then *wow... Just wow.* The view here was tremendous.

"Ma'am?"

The cowboy maintained a firm, steadying grip on her arm. For which she was grateful.

"Yay!" The little cowboy fist-pumped the air. "You didn't kill her."

Using the cowboy as a counterbalance, she carefully got to her feet. The dress didn't make it easy.

She blushed. "Reports of my death have been greatly exaggerated."

"I'm so sorry, ma'am. I didn't see you. I did everything I could not to hit you—"

"You didn't hit me."

She gazed into his face. He must be well over six feet tall. Underneath the fleece-lined Carhartt jacket, he was a big man with broad shoulders. His sheer handsomeness took her breath.

If there was one thing she knew, it was clothes. But unlike most of her male acquaintances, the clothes didn't make this man. Rather, it was the other way around.

"Not your fault. I fainted. Thankfully, I didn't hit my head. I'm fine."

He smelled good, too. Something woodsy with notes of leather and hay.

So she did what she did when she didn't know what else to do—she babbled.

"I don't usually faint, but I haven't eaten anything today. Actually, I haven't eaten anything in about forty-eight hours. But I couldn't, you see. My stomach was simply tied in knots."

Brow furrowed, the cowboy eyeballed her like he'd never seen her species before. She wasn't unused to such reactions from men.

The little cowboy tucked his small hand through the crook of her arm. "I wike her, Dad, don't you?"

Dad? She wilted. *Oh.*

The cowboy was married. *Of course, he's married, AnnaBeth. Are you an idiot?* This hunk of man had to have been lassoed into matrimony long, long ago.

"Sweet potatoes," she muttered.

"Excuse me, ma'am?"

She disentangled herself from his grasp. *Off-limits, AnnaBeth.* She was delusional to have imagined someone like her unremarkable, big-hipped self could ever find herself rescued by someone tall, blond *and* available.

AnnaBeth motioned toward her vehicle, which was rapidly disappearing under a mantle of falling snow. "My car broke down. And before that, I got lost."

Little Cowboy hadn't let go of her arm, but she didn't mind. It was nice. He was like a human muff. And so, so cute.

The cowboy's deep brown eyes sharpened. "Where were you headed?"

"Nowhere. Anywhere. I mean, I hadn't planned much beyond getting out of town. 'Head west, young man,' they used to say. So I guess I decided to take their advice. Except in my case, it would've been 'head west, young woman,' you see." Taking a quick breath, she touched her hand to where the gigantic bow had dipped over one eye. "You do see, don't you?"

It was only after the words left her mouth, she realized how nonsensical she must sound. His gaze held a hint of alarm.

Her stomach tightened. Yet how could she hope to say anything sensible with his handsome self staring at her like that?

Chapter Two

Jonas was beginning to believe that maybe she *had* hit her head. She didn't look like a criminal on the lam, but what did he know? As his mother was quick to remind him, he didn't get out much.

Of course, the woman being a flatlander could possibly explain the absurdity of the situation. Flatlanders did illogical and ill-advised things.

Like driving an expensive sports car on a mountain in a blinding snowstorm. His eyes cut to the enormous bow on her head. In a fancy, pre-Christmas party getup, no less.

Unlike the usual mountain twang he was accustomed to, she spoke in one of those soft, honeyed Southern drawls.

The pretty flatlander smiled at him. Brightly. Those eyes of hers…

She held out her hand. "Where are my manners? We haven't been introduced. My name is AnnaBeth Cummings."

"I know." He shoved the purse at her. "I needed a name to tell the paramedics." He stuck his hands in his coat pockets. "Although, I doubt they'd have made it up the mountain in these conditions."

The flatlander blinked at him. Once. Twice. "And your name would be?"

"Jonas Stone."

Hunter swung around to face her. "My name's Hunter."

Jonas didn't like how his son hadn't let go of the woman. As if he was already getting too attached.

The Cummings woman touched a light hand to the top of his son's small Stetson. "I like your hat." She tilted her head. The floppy bow went cattywampus again. "So much better than mine."

Hunter grinned. "I'm a cowboy." He jutted his thumb. "Wike my dad."

She smiled. "I can see that."

The flatlander had a nice smile.

"We have a wanch. And hosses. Most people visit us in the summer."

She glanced at Jonas.

"FieldStone Dude Ranch."

"A real ranch with real cowboys." She threw him another smile. "How fun."

The sweetness of her smile sent him into a tailspin, and he felt the need to be disagreeable. "It's a lot of hard work."

Her smile faltered. "Thank you for coming to my rescue, Mr. Stone. I hate to trouble you further, but perhaps you could call a tow truck for me?" She squeezed Hunter's hand before letting go. "I can wait in my car until it arrives."

She had an expressive face. He wondered what it must be like to wear your feelings so transparently for everyone to see. Somebody ought to warn her.

The world loved nothing better than squashing little optimists like her. He ought to know. Once upon a time, he'd been one, too.

"No, Dad…" Hunter's eyes beseeched him. "She's supposed to come home wif us."

Confusion flitted across the woman's face. "Supposed?"

"If the paramedics can't make it here tonight, a tow truck can't, either." Jonas folded his arms over his chest. "You can't stay in your car. You'll freeze to death."

What was he going to do with her? There was nothing on this road, except the ranch. He doubted he could take her to town and return before the road became impassable. He didn't like the idea of leaving his mother isolated at the ranch. And he had the horses to think of, too.

"I'm sure I'll be fine." The honey in her voice became crisp, businesslike. "Don't let me keep you."

Shards of ice pelted the shoulders of his jacket. He sighed. Loudly.

"Look, lady. There's nothing else for it."

This was giving him a headache. He scowled. The entire day had turned into a giant headache.

"You'll have to spend the night at the lodge, Miz Cummings."

Her chin came up. "It's 'Miss.' But please call me AnnaBeth." She bit her lip. "I don't want to impose. Or be a bother."

Something slightly woebegone in her voice stirred his conscience. Not the most gracious of invitations. Grown or not, had his mother heard him, she would've tanned his hide.

But he was tired. And there was something about this woman that made him...

Hunter's gaze ping-ponged from his father to the flatlander. "D-Dad?" His little guy's voice quavered.

And what about the ungentlemanly—not to mention un-Christian—example he was setting for his son?

So when life started whirling out of control, he did what he usually did: he got exasperated. "Everyone, just get in the truck."

Hunter solemnly pursed his mouth. "Don't fo-get to say pwease, Dad."

Jonas gritted his teeth. "*Please* get in the truck."

She took a step toward her car. "My suitcase."

He caught the sleeve of her coat. "I'll get it. Trunk or passenger seat?"

"Trunk. And a smaller bag, too." She snapped open her purse, and handed him the key. "Thank you, Mr. Stone."

"Jonas," he muttered.

She gave him a small smile, but big enough to launch a storm of another kind square in the middle of his chest.

He stomped through the growing drifts to her vehicle. He wasn't usually given to such frivolous notions, but the flatlander seemed to bring out the nonsensical in him.

After relocking her car, he stowed the pink, hard-shell case and the smaller black camera bag below Hunter's dangling boots. Once behind the steering wheel, he found himself shoulder-to-shoulder with a blushing AnnaBeth.

Straddling the transmission console, she sat squashed between Hunter's booster seat and the wheel. "Sorry," she whispered.

Thing was, part of him was real sorry. And the other part…wasn't. The part that enjoyed the pleasing scent of roses wafting from her.

He glowered at the pleased part of himself.

She gazed through the windshield. "It's really coming down. I've never seen so much snow in my life. Autumn at this elevation must be spectacular. It's my favorite season."

His favorite season, too. But it was becoming apparent she didn't require his contribution to keep a conversation going. Which was more than fine with him. Instead, he cranked up the heat a notch.

She positioned her heels together on the hump underneath the vent. "Despite being cold and barren, I think winter is beautiful in it's own way."

Cold and barren—not unlike his life since Kasey left. He'd lost more than his marriage. He'd lost his hope. Like a horse in the trace, he'd kept his head down, his heart bridled, and plodded on. Existing day-to-day.

"Is the ranch far?"

He gripped the wheel. "Not far." The truck plowed through the blowing drifts. There was a brief silence, and then—

"Think we'll make it?"

He flicked a glance at her. She was as perky and bubbly as a brand-new pup. And about as much trouble.

Jonas set his jaw. "Yes."

"Not much of a talker, are you?"

Hunching his shoulders, he gave her a sideways look. "Not something I imagine you've ever been accused of."

She laughed.

AnnaBeth Cummings had a nice laugh. Light, happy and silvery. He almost smiled…before he caught himself.

Perhaps giving him up as a lost cause—she wouldn't be the first—she turned to his son. They spent the next few minutes discussing weighty matters, such as a preference for peanut butter or chocolate. They decided on both.

Ahead, he spotted the familiar stone pillars marking the entrance to the ranch. Nearly home. He couldn't wait to off-load the high-spirited flatlander onto his mother.

God willing—and the creek didn't freeze—come tomorrow this unsettling woman would return to her own world. And he could return to his.

The idea failed to cheer him as much as he'd supposed it might. He had the disquieting feeling that somehow nothing might ever be the same again.

Once through the FieldStone gateposts, the land opened into a valley of wood-framed cabins. AnnaBeth leaned forward to get a better view. A blanket of snow lay over everything. Snow-daubed evergreens dotted the perimeter of the property.

"It's like something out of a dream," she said. "A dream of home, family and belonging."

Jonas Stone's eyes cut to her. Cheeks reddening, she set her face forward.

With great excitement, Hunter drew her attention to points of interest. The truck wound its way over the rolling terrain, past the split-rail fence that lined the snow-covered pastures.

She waved her hand. "I love the names of the cabins." She savored the words. "The Laurel. The Azalea. The Hummingbird."

Hunter hugged her arm. "I'm so happy you're fine-a-wee here."

"Finally here?" Touched by the sweet sincerity in the little boy's face, she hugged him back. "So am I, sweetie pie."

"Uh…" Jonas shifted. "Miss Cummings… My son…" An interesting look she wasn't sure how to interpret fell across his features.

She smiled at him. "Yes, Mr. Stone?"

But his face resumed its usual aloof expression. "Nothing…"

She bit her lip. Reminding herself that not everyone enjoyed conversation, she concentrated on his son. "Why is the ranch called the FieldStone, Hunter?"

"My name is Stone." Hunter broadened his chest. "And Gwam-ma's name is Fielding."

Jonas drummed his thumbs on the steering wheel. "I'm the fourth-generation Stone to work the ranch."

Hunter held up his small hand. "I'll be... One, two, three, four." He ticked off each finger. "Five."

She tapped her finger on the tip of his button nose. "Yes, you will be."

Jonas cleared his throat. "When my father died—"

"Oh." She straightened. "I'm so sorry."

Jonas shrugged. "I was too young to remember him."

"I was young when my mother died, too."

His stoic expression flickered for a second before the impenetrable barrier fell into place once more. "My mother married the ranch foreman, Wilton Fielding."

"Field... Stone." She smiled. "Got it."

"He was great," Jonas grunted. "Best stepfather I could've wished for."

She settled her back against the seat. Unlike when her father married pushy Victoria, who, in her opinion, left a lot to be desired in the mothering department.

"Dat's the Whip-po-wheel." Hunter motioned toward the duplex cabin. "And over dere's de Dogwood."

Jonas never took his eyes from the road. "Whippoor-will."

Hunter gestured to the red, gambrel-roofed barn. "We have dances dere."

At the curve in the bend of trees, his father palmed the wheel. "In summer."

The hunky cowboy might not be much of a talker, but he had nice hands. Lived-in hands. Strong, work-calloused hands. When he caught her looking, she felt a blush creep up her neck.

Get it through your head, AnnaBeth. He's married.

Although—she cut her eyes to his hands again—he wasn't wearing a ring. But what did she know? Maybe some married men didn't.

"Sweet potatoes," she muttered, earning her another unreadable glance from Jonas.

"Haywides and twail wides and hoss-shoes." Hunter motioned toward two tall poles, standing like steel sentinels on the snow-packed concrete. "And va-wee-bawl."

Twilight was descending fast. But on a knoll above the cluster of cabins and outbuildings, lights from a two-story wood-and-stone structure beckoned.

Hunter grinned. "We're home."

AnnaBeth gulped. Home. She'd done more than just run away from her own wedding.

She'd spent her entire life trying to please her father. He'd been so ecstatic about her engagement. It made her sick to think of how she'd disappointed him today.

And after embarrassing Victoria in front of

Charlotte society, she doubted she had a home anymore. She'd learned early not to make waves. Now she'd pay a heavy price for asserting her independence.

Pulling the truck into the circular driveway in front of the house, Jonas parked at the end of the snow-covered sidewalk. When he got out, the wind whistled through the open door, and she shuddered.

"Wait here." He grimaced. "I'll come around."

She tried not to take his unfriendliness to heart. "Do you need help unbuckling the lap belt, Hunter?"

"I can do it." He pressed the lever, and the belt whizzed free, retracting. "I'm a big boy."

She smiled. "Yes, you are."

Keeping his thumb down, he held up his hand. "I'm four."

"So, so big," she agreed.

His father threw open the door and stepped aside as Hunter jumped to the ground. "Miss Cummings?"

Ignoring his outstretched hand, she slid across the seat and inched around the booster seat. At the edge of the cab, she hesitated. He took hold of her hand.

The moment his fingers touched her skin, sparks flew up her arm. His brown eyes widened. Mirroring, she figured, her own shock.

"Static electricity," he muttered.

Of course. What else could it be? Discombobulated, she allowed him to assist her to the ground. Her heels sank into the snow.

Dropping his hand, she took a step forward. Snow sloshed inside her open-toed, ivory silk pumps. At the sudden cold, she gasped.

She slogged forward, but it was slow going. Gauging the distance from the truck to the house, she bit back a sigh. She was beginning to lose feeling in her feet. Her knees wobbled.

He flicked a look in her direction. "Miss Cummings?"

"M-m-maybe you sh-sh-should go first and warn your w-w-wife to expect c-c-company."

Giving her a dour look, he folded his arms over his chest. "I don't have a wife."

Maybe that's just what his face did whenever he looked at her. Then his words registered.

The hunky cowboy didn't have a wife.

"Don't want a wife," he growled.

The small, irrepressible bubble of joy burst. Another dream dying an ignominious death. But that meant Jonas Stone was a widower? Or divorced?

Hunter tugged her hand. "My mudder died, too, Snow Pwincess."

"I'm not a princess— Whoa!"

Jonas scooped her into his arms.

Sucking in a breath, she found herself pressed

against the softness of his calfskin coat. "What're you doing?"

"Getting you out of the cold before you get pneumonia." He plowed forward.

Jostled, she threw her arms around his neck. He'd lifted her so effortlessly, thinking nothing of it. As if she was MaryDru or Victoria.

"I'll get your bags later."

She found herself at eye level with his square, stubble-covered jaw. A vein pulsed in his throat, visible in the exposed *V* of skin where he'd neglected to fasten the top button of his coat. But he fixed his gaze on navigating the slippery path.

Hunter didn't wait for them. Racing along the sidewalk, he headed for the porch. The heavy oak door swung open. A cell phone in her hand, an attractive, auburn-haired woman in her late fifties ventured out.

"Look what Santa bwought me, Gwam-ma!" Hunter bobbed in his boots. "Me and Dad bwung her home."

Jonas carried AnnaBeth up the stone steps.

"I was on the phone with Aunt IdaLee…" Eyes the same shade as the cowboy's, his mother's gaze darted from her grandson to AnnaBeth. "Who have you brought home, Jonas?"

AnnaBeth pushed the obnoxious bow higher on her forehead. "Mr. Stone rescued me on the mountain road after my car broke down."

Tucking the phone into the pocket of her cardigan, Mrs. Fielding ushered them inside the house.

"She was walking on the woad, Gwam-ma. Dad awe-most killed her."

Mrs. Fielding shut the door against the driving snow. "What?"

"A misunderstanding." Keeping one arm draped around his neck for balance, she held out her hand. "I'm AnnaBeth Cummings. So sorry to drop in on you like this."

"Please call me Deirdre." Eyes narrowing, his mother clasped her fingers. "AnnaBeth Cummings... Why does your name sound so familiar?" An amused expression lightened her features. "Speaking of dropped, feel free to put her down anytime, Jonas."

The color of his neck immediately went brick-red. He set AnnaBeth on her feet so fast, she had to catch hold of the wall.

"Sorry to be so heavy," she whispered.

"You're not heavy. I'm used to hauling sacks of feed." He scrubbed his hand over his face. "Not that you're like a sack of feed... Or any other kind of sack... I just meant..." He closed his eyes. "I'm going to stop talking now."

His mother planted her hands on her hips. "Silence might be for the best, Jonas."

"I'll go get your luggage." A flush darkening

his sharp cheekbones, he slipped out the door and back into the storm.

"Please forgive my inarticulate son." Deirdre led AnnaBeth into a large, open-space living room. "He's rusty when it comes to a woman's tender sensibilities."

Rough-hewn wooden beams bolstered the soaring ceiling. A wall of windows provided what in fair weather she guessed were magnificent views of the Blue Ridge Mountains.

Deirdre eased AnnaBeth into one of the leather armchairs flanking the massive stone fireplace. Orange-red flames danced from the fire in the hearth.

"Thank you, Deirdre."

At the sudden whoosh of cold air, Jonas returned. Using his shoulder, he heaved the stout oak door shut, cutting off the roaring wind.

Hunter plastered himself to AnnaBeth's elbow. "I told her awe about de wanch, Gwam-ma."

Deirdre smiled, tiny lines fanning out from the corners of her eyes. "Welcome to the FieldStone Ranch, AnnaBeth." She nudged the brim of Hunter's Stetson upward. "Hats off in the house, remember, Hunter?"

AnnaBeth liked the motherly Deirdre Fielding. Probably not her fault that her son was a surly, ill-tempered cowboy.

Shuffling his boots, Jonas handed Hunter his

hat, too. Hunter hung both hats on pegs on the far wall.

Deirdre's gaze fell to AnnaBeth. "Oh, honey. You must be frozen. We need to get you out of those wet clothes. And those shoes... Your feet must feel like a block of ice." She turned to her son. "How long was she walking in the snow? We should check for frostbite."

"F-frostbite?" she whispered.

All of a sudden, everything became too much. The wedding. Scott. MaryDru. Getting lost. Almost getting hit by a truck.

Now this? Her eyelids stung with unshed tears. Hunter, Jonas and Mrs. Fielding swam in her vision.

By running away, had she made the worst mistake of her life?

Chapter Three

Jonas could stand a lot of things, but not a woman's tears.

Ducking out from under the strap of Anna-Beth's camera bag, he set both cases at the base of the staircase. "Let me check for signs of frostbite." He dropped onto the leather ottoman in front of her chair. Hunter hovered at his side.

"It won't be long before dinner." His mother moved toward the kitchen at the back of the lodge. "But we need to get something warm inside her now. Do you like coffee, AnnaBeth, honey?"

AnnaBeth started to rise. "Yes, but you mustn't wait on—"

"Lots of sugar, Mom, for shock." A hand on her arm, he eased her onto the cushions. "We don't want her fainting again."

A line puckered AnnaBeth's otherwise perfect brow. "But—"

His mother had already gone.

Jonas felt sick thinking of what could've happened to AnnaBeth if he and Hunter hadn't come along when they did. In the Blue Ridge, winter should never be taken for granted.

"Son, can you find some socks to keep her feet warm?"

"Yes, sir." Boots clattering, Hunter dashed upstairs.

She lowered her gaze to her hands, clasped in her lap. "I don't usually take my coffee with sugar. As a general rule, I don't eat sugar. I mean, I try to avoid it."

AnnaBeth twisted a button on her coat. "I've always had to watch my weight. I really don't need any sugar."

He sensed a lifetime of hurt in her words. And none of it true. She was taller than average, about five foot six to his six foot three. But she fit perfectly well in his arms. Far too well for his peace of mind.

Jonas frowned. "Who told you that you should watch your weight?"

She tucked her chin into the collar of her coat. "Daddy says I take after my mother. But Victoria said I was just big-boned, and I needed to watch my carbs." Two spots of red burned in her cheeks.

His gut knotted. He didn't know her father or Victoria—nor was he likely to—but on general principle he decided he didn't like them. Not if they'd hurt AnnaBeth.

Although, hadn't he done the same insensitive thing? Remorse flooded him. He recalled her earlier apology for being too heavy. And his response.

He scrubbed his hand over his face. He should be horsewhipped. His mother was right. He'd turned into a curmudgeon. An idiot who didn't know how to treat a lady.

Open mouth, insert horseshoe. Actually, the entire horse—saddle and blanket, too. Which reminded him… He stood.

Startled, her gaze lifted to his and locked. For a second, his world went sideways. Blood pounded in his ears.

Only by sheer force of will did he direct his feet toward the sofa. He must've risen too fast. Made himself dizzy.

Snatching the afghan off the sofa, he resumed his seat on the ottoman. "Prop your feet on my knees."

Eyelashes fluttering like the wings of a frightened bird, she pursed her lips. "What? Why?"

What's wrong with you? Manners, Jonas. Even four-year-old Hunter knew the magic words.

"Please." He opened his hands. "I need to make sure your toes don't have frostbite."

"A-all right."

She lifted first one foot and then the other. He was appalled—and scared—at how blue her feet appeared. Why on earth had she ventured out in such inappropriate footwear?

Gently, he eased off her left shoe, and set it on the floor beside them. Next, he removed the right one.

His thumb accidentally brushed against the skin on top of her foot. She quivered. His throat clogged. Her feet were cold, so cold, but thank You, God, no signs of frostbite.

Jonas wrapped her lower limbs in the folds of the afghan. Through the fabric, he rubbed the circulation back into her feet.

Her cheeks turned a bright shade of pink. "You don't have to do that, Mr. Stone."

Pausing, he frowned. "I told you, it's Jonas."

She fidgeted in the chair. "You don't have to do that. I'll be fine. I *am* fine, J-Jonas…"

Was saying his name that difficult?

He glared. "Be still, woman. The storm out there is nothing to play around with. The Blue Ridge Mountains are beautiful, but they can also be deadly."

As beautiful as AnnaBeth Cummings. The thought stopped him cold. Momentarily befuddled, he stared at her.

Her lips parted. "What's wrong?"

Nothing. Everything. His mother returned to the living room, bringing him back to the present.

She handed AnnaBeth a coffee mug. "Cream and sugar."

AnnaBeth's face fell. "Thank you." Dutifully, she brought the mug to her lips.

He squeezed her foot. "Not that you should worry, but the cream and sugar don't count today."

AnnaBeth arched an eyebrow. "They don't?"

"Not when it's the first thing you've eaten in forty-eight hours." He rubbed the back of his neck. "You said... On the road..."

"I didn't think you were listening. Most people—" Averting her gaze, she took a big gulp of coffee and sputtered. "Wow. That's strong. But good," she added quickly.

Jonas had noticed that about her. Always so careful not to give the slightest offense. Yet with that red hair of hers, he wondered what she'd be like if she ever got mad. Did she ever allow herself to get mad?

His mother smiled. "My coffee's like my two cowboys. Strong. Sometimes a little thick. But with undertones of sweetness."

Jonas started to rise, but his mother waved him to remain where he was. "Look's like you've got this under control." She settled onto the nearby sofa. "Like I said, a little thick. At least at first."

Hunter dashed downstairs, saving him from further comment. "Here you go, Snow Pwincess."

AnnaBeth blushed. "I'm not— Why don't you call me AnnaBeth, Hunter? Or A.B. That's what my sister, MaryDru, calls me." She set the mug on the side table.

Hunter jutted his jaw. "I'd wather caw you—"

"Son!" Jonas got to his feet so fast, the room spun. Again. "Give Miss AnnaBeth the socks."

A pleased expression flitted across her features. And he realized it was the first time he'd said her name out loud. Although, he'd been thinking her name far longer.

Kasey used to complain he was emotionally unavailable. How she never knew what he was thinking. After she deserted them, probably better she hadn't.

Hunter thrust the socks at AnnaBeth. "Dese awe so, so wawrm, Miss AnnaBef."

Jonas narrowed his eyes. "Where did you get those, Hunter?"

His son grinned. "Dese socks keep your feet wawrm, Dad. You told me to go get socks."

Jonas ran his hand over his head. "I meant for you to get a pair from Gramma's room, Hunt."

Bending, AnnaBeth slipped on the heather-gray, wool boot socks. "Already my toes feel toastier." She sighed. "I'm in love."

He gave her a startled glance.

She went crimson. "I mean I'm in love with these socks." She stuck out her feet.

Deirdre snapped her fingers. Everyone jumped. "That's where I've seen your name. You write the *Heart's Home* blog. I love your tagline." She smiled. "'May your heart always know the way home.' That's you, isn't it, AnnaBeth?"

"That's me." She tucked a strand of hair behind her ear. "Do you enjoy the blog, Deirdre?"

Hunter planted his fists on his pint-sized hips. "What's a bwog?"

"Something on the computer." Jonas jammed his hands in the pockets of his jeans. "That's what you do for a living? You write a blog?"

AnnaBeth lifted her chin. "I'm an influencer."

Jonas blinked. "A what?"

"Honestly, son." His mom threw out her hands. "Get off the mountain once in a while. Even if virtually. AnnaBeth Cummings writes reviews for products. She's a trendsetter."

AnnaBeth fluttered her hand. "I only write about what I love."

"I loved your 'Autumn Wardrobe Must-Have' post a few months ago. And the endorsement you wrote for the Duer Inn sounded wonderful. Somewhere in Virginia?"

AnnaBeth nodded. "The Eastern Shore. A great place. Fantastic people. If you've never been, you should go."

His mother's lips curved. "Looked like a great place for a honeymoon."

AnnaBeth's cheeks turned pink.

He crossed his arms. *Obvious much, Mother?*

Jonas glowered. "I'll take your cases upstairs. Which room, Ma?"

"I was thinking the Snowbird." His mother headed to the staircase. "It's an en-suite corner room, AnnaBeth, with a lovely view of the ridge."

"Not that she can see the ridge in this weather," he growled. "No telling when the storm will let up."

AnnaBeth batted her lashes. "Are you always this cheerful and optimistic, Jonas?"

His mother laughed. "I think I'm going to adore having you around, AnnaBeth."

Jonas scowled at them both.

"Stay by the fire for a few more minutes, Anna-Beth, and finish your coffee." Climbing the stairs, his mother called over her shoulder, "I'll put clean towels in the bathroom."

Hunter grabbed the suitcase. "De Snowbirwd for de Snow Pwincess."

"Take it easy, little dude." He took the case from his son. "That's too heavy for you."

Hunter reached for the camera bag, but Jonas beat him to it. "Best leave that to me, too, son."

If Hunter lost his grip and the bag tumbled down the staircase, the lens might shatter.

Hunter poked out his lip. "I'm big. I'm a cowboy." Injured pride shone out of his earnest little face. As did the beginning signs of a fit of temper.

AnnaBeth leaned forward. "Such a big cowboy, sweetie pie. And a good helper."

Hunter's indignation deflated a notch.

She tapped her finger to her chin. "I'm sure your dad will need your help later. Maybe right now, though, you could help Gramma put out the towels. Can you do that for me, sweetie pie?"

"I can do dat, Miss AnnaBef." Hunter bobbed on the tips of his boots. "You're going to be so happy here." His forehead creased. "You won't go anywhere while I'm gone, will you?"

She touched his cheek in a gesture so sweet, Jonas's breath hitched.

"I'll be right here, little cowboy."

Hunter's face lit. "I've been waiting for you a long, long time, Miss AnnaBef. My whole—"

Jonas cleared his throat. "Run upstairs and help Gramma, Hunt."

Hunter raced for the stairs.

"Thanks for that, AnnaBeth." Jonas kept his gaze trained on the upper story until Hunter disappeared from view. "He doesn't usually get so cranky, but it's been a long day. He's tired and hungry."

"I remember when my sister, MaryDru, was

little." AnnaBeth smiled. "Tired and hungry is a perilous combination."

Right now, Jonas felt in peril. Peril that had nothing to do with a snowstorm or a preschooler. He hefted the suitcase and camera bag.

She'd said the ranch reminded her of a dream. Home, family and belonging. Is that what Anna-Beth Cummings dreamed of?

It was a dream he'd spent his entire life trying to create for himself and Hunter at the Field-Stone. A dream Kasey hadn't shared. Emptiness gnawed at his chest, in the place where his heart used to reside, leaving him feeling hollowed-out and free-falling.

What was with him?

Time to put some distance between himself and the flatlander. As much distance as he could while snowbound inside the lodge. He started toward the relative safety of the second floor.

But with a sinking feeling, he wondered when it came to the alluring AnnaBeth Cummings if distance alone would cure what suddenly ailed him.

AnnaBeth wasn't sure what she'd said that set off Jonas, but he'd hightailed it upstairs with her cases like she'd lit his hair on fire.

Getting out of the comfy chair, she edged toward the window. Outside, the storm continued to rage. She sighed. Considering the whiteout conditions, she might be forced to impose on Jonas Stone and his less-than-enthusiastic hospitality longer than anyone had anticipated.

And there was the matter of her car. What was she going to do about her car? Even after she got it fixed, what then?

She'd planned on moving into Scott's condo after the wedding, so she'd relinquished her apartment in Charlotte. At this moment, she was essentially homeless.

But ever the optimist, she rallied. Life could be a whole lot worse than being trapped in a luxurious lodge in front of a cozy fire with Hunter the little cowboy, the motherly Deirdre Fielding and Jonas, the hunky but unfriendly cowboy for company.

Yeah, like I could be married to a man in love with my sister. Or still lost on a remote mountain road in a blizzard. Chased by wolves... Eaten by bears...

If Jonas Stone hadn't come along, no one might have known what happened to her. She'd have been missing, presumed dead by her family.

Until her frozen corpse was found after the spring thaw. Maybe even by Jonas. Then he'd be sorry for being so snarly...

Although, if he'd never come along in the first place, he could hardly have regrets. She shook herself.

Whatever. No point in interrupting a great story—based on real events—with the facts. MaryDru jokingly claimed that, despite not being biologically related, it was AnnaBeth who'd acquired Victoria's flair for the dramatic.

Sinking once more into the cushion, she propped her chin in her hand. Maybe she should consider adding a podcast next year to *Heart's Home*…

"Mom's got your room ready, AnnaBeth."

Jolted, her chin fell out of her hand. Jonas, minus the heavy coat, stood beside the chair.

"Sorry," he muttered. "I thought you heard me come downstairs." He rolled his shirtsleeves to his elbows and revealed forearms thickly corded with muscle.

Both of them turned at the sound of Hunter clomping down the steps.

Jonas made a wry face. "No mistaking *him*, is there?"

Her lips curving, she wagged her finger at Jonas. "Don't talk about my favorite little guy like that."

The little cowboy tromped over. "Hey, Miss AnnaBef." He grinned.

She ruffled his short-cropped hair, and unfolded from the chair. "Your mother mentioned dinner. I can help out."

Jonas rubbed his jaw. "I think she's got it under

control, so you've got time to change into dry clothes. Let me take your coat."

"Um…" She bit her lip. "My coat?"

Jonas gave her a quizzical look. "Yes, your coat."

Wiping her hands on a dish towel, Deirdre emerged from the rear of the lodge.

Jonas held out his hand. "I'll hang your coat in the mudroom off the kitchen." The family, including little Hunter, looked at her, waiting.

So with great reluctance, AnnaBeth unbuttoned her coat and slipped her arms out of the sleeves. Letting his hand drop, Jonas gave an audible gasp.

Deirdre pursed her lips. "Well, that explains the bow."

AnnaBeth pushed the bow out of her eyes.

Hunter fingered one of the floating ruffles flaring out below her knees. "Soft." He smiled at his dad. "She is pwetty, isn't she, Dad?"

Jonas's eyes darkened. "Why are you wearing a wedding dress, AnnaBeth?"

"'Cause she's a snow bwide, Dad. Our snow—"

"Hunter."

She winced at Jonas's clipped tone.

From the sudden chill in his manner, she could well imagine what he thought of her. Flighty. Shallow. Harebrained. Lacking substance. Or worth.

He wouldn't be the first. Her family—with the

exception of MaryDru—were charter members of the Don't-Be-Ridiculous-AnnaBeth club.

Deirdre swallowed. "Oh, honey. On top of everything else that happened today, it was supposed to be your wedding day, too?"

AnnaBeth's cheeks flamed. "It sure hasn't turned out to be the day I expected."

His face inscrutable, Jonas stepped back a pace. "Where's your groom?"

She bit her lip. "Back in Charlotte."

Jonas and his mother exchanged glances.

Deirdre patted Hunter's shoulder. "Why don't you help me set the table for dinner? You can put out a special place for AnnaBeth."

He smiled. "Okay, Gwam-ma. I'm so happy you're here early, Miss AnnaBef." He hugged her legs.

Early? Not daring to look at his father, she wrapped her arms around Hunter, inhaling the sweet little-boy scent of him.

Jonas pulled at his arm. "Go with Gramma, Hunt. Please."

Letting go of her, Hunter followed his grandmother beyond the long pine table in the adjacent dining area toward the door AnnaBeth guessed led to the lodge kitchen.

Jonas took the coat from her. "AnnaBeth?"

She chewed the inside of her cheek. She really didn't want to get into what had happened between her, Scott and MaryDru. She didn't have the emotional energy to go into it. Her wedding debacle wasn't any of his business.

And then Jonas Stone surprised her.

"The guy's a total jerk to have jilted you at the altar," Jonas said, his gravelly voice slightly fierce. "You know that, right?"

Scott jilting *her* wasn't exactly what took place. She opened her mouth to correct Jonas, but stopped. After declaring his love for her sister, that was exactly what Scott had been about to do. Only she'd beaten him to the punch and run away first. Jonas didn't need to know the embarrassing details of her never-got-off-the-ground marriage.

Despite evidence to the contrary, she still had a few tattered remnants of pride. Everyone who mattered already knew what happened. Anyone else was on a need-to-know basis. And Jonas fell into the category of "most definitely didn't need to know."

Besides, give or take twenty-four hours, she'd never see him again. That thought descended upon her with unexpected gloom. But Jonas wasn't done surprising her.

"Small consolation—trust me, I know—but you're better off without him." Her coat clutched in his large hands, he wrung the garment as if he wished it was Scott's neck. "You're better off not hitched to a loser like him for the rest of your life."

A curious mixture of simmering fury—not directed at her, but on her behalf—and compassion filled his dark eyes. She gaped at him. And reminded herself to breathe.

No one had ever defended her supposedly injured honor so vigorously before.

"Don't worry about your car. My cousin, Zach, owns the auto-repair shop in Truelove. I'll get him to tow your car and find out what's wrong."

She didn't know what to say. And for once, surprising herself, she said nothing.

But like a bottle finally uncorked, Jonas continued to speak.

"Storm's likely to last all night, but until the roads are plowed, no one can get on or off the mountain. Worst-case scenario, we could be snowed in here for a few days." A muscle jumped in his jaw. "We'll sort everything out. I promise."

A veritable avalanche of words. Jonas would be exhausted tomorrow, no doubt.

She wasn't sure what had prompted his about-face. He said he knew—as in understood first-hand?—that she was better off without her erstwhile groom. In the past, had something equally humiliating and hurtful happened to him, too?

Jonas squared his shoulders. Broad shoulders that tapered to a narrow waist, where his shirttail was tucked into his jeans. "Stay here as long as you like, AnnaBeth. You've found a safe place, a refuge from the storm, here with us at the Field-Stone."

Her heart gave a funny quiver. Her eyes locked with his. She soon became lost in his melted-chocolate eyes.

But truth be told, she was lost in more ways than just the obvious.

Chapter Four

After gulping down a quick cup of coffee the next morning, Jonas headed outside to feed the horses before breakfast. On the terrace, he paused to take in the wintry panorama of the ranch.

On the horizon, the surrounding mountain peaks undulated like cresting waves of snow. The precipitation had ended sometime during the wee hours. And sunrise dawned with a crisp, clear beauty. So beautiful it took his breath.

Not unlike the runaway bride he and Hunter had stumbled upon yesterday.

Frowning, he pushed off the patio. He was already regretting what he'd said to AnnaBeth last night. And what he'd inadvertently let slip about himself. But unhappy memories had resurfaced when he realized she'd been jilted at the altar.

He could well imagine her humiliation on what was supposed to be the most wonderful day of her life. How heartbroken she must be. How forsaken she must feel.

Something pinged inside his chest. He clenched his jaw. AnnaBeth wasn't his responsibility.

Inside the horse barn, he stomped his boots to dislodge the snow. After breakfast, he needed to work on clearing the winding ranch driveway. And call his cousin, Zach. Although, no time like the present...

He blew on his hands before digging his cell phone out of his pocket. Only after several rings did he realize how early it was. Zach might not be—

"Sorry to wake you, Zach. It's Jonas."

"Dude..." His cousin grunted. "Ranchers aren't the only ones running a business. I've been up since the storm moved on, towing vehicles all over town that slid off the road or got stuck in the snow."

"Actually, that's why I'm calling." Jonas remembered something else. "Oh, and since you live in town, Mom wanted me to ask you to check on Aunt IdaLee. Make sure she didn't lose electricity. That she has enough firewood—"

"I'm headed over there right now. She's got pancakes and sausage waiting for me."

Their aunt IdaLee was over eighty and had never married. But over the course of her five-decade teaching career, she'd taught nearly everyone in the county. Between all her grown-up former pupils and extended family, Truelove made sure she was well looked after.

A few years younger than Jonas, Zach was a skinny beanpole of a fellow. With a bottomless stomach and NASCAR aspirations.

"Once you've filled your belly, cousin, there's this broken-down vehicle on our—"

"I heard about your stranded snow princess." Zach snickered.

Jonas could probably thank his mother for that. After dinner, he'd seen her on the phone.

He grimaced. "Her name is AnnaBeth Cummings. Did Aunt IdaLee tell you what happened?"

"Nope. When Miss GeorgeAnne opened the hardware store this morning, she told me. She's doing a booming business selling snow shovels and sleds. Apparently, Miss GeorgeAnne, Aunt IdaLee and Miss ErmaJean had a conference call last night."

Flashing back to how ErmaJean the elf had overheard Hunter's Santa wish, he bit back a groan. "Don't tell me those old women are already conspiring."

"You definitely have a bull's-eye painted on your back, cuz."

"She's not my snow bride," he growled.

"Better you than me, dude. You don't know how happy I am to not be you." Zach gave a less-than-sympathetic laugh. "But no can do on towing the car today. The mountain road won't be clear 'til tomorrow. Until then, for better or for worse, the snow bride is all yours." He chortled. "Did you see what I did there? Better or worse?"

Jonas clenched his teeth so tight his jaw ached. "We'll see how hard you're laughing when I tell Aunt IdaLee it was you playing with matches that caught the Christmas tree on fire that year."

"I was six!" Zach huffed. "Don't go getting your spurs in a twist. Whatcha so afraid of? You got no call to be so—"

Jonas ended the call and scrubbed his face. *Was* he scared of the flatlander? The thought of her emerald-green eyes was like a punch to his gut.

Yep, 'fraid so. Something about AnnaBeth completely addled him. Call him a coward, but a little fear was healthy, right?

He headed toward the stalls. The sooner he could get AnnaBeth on her merry way, the better off he'd be. Until then?

If he had to stay outside all day, he'd do his best to avoid her. Out of sight, out of mind.

Famous last words?

It was the light filtering through the gingham curtain that awakened AnnaBeth. Curled beneath the gorgeous blue-and-white quilt, she felt as cozy as a cat. And as reluctant to move.

A kaleidoscope of yesterday's events bombarded her memory. Scott and MaryDru. Her frantic flight, the snowstorm and the subsequent rescue by Jonas.

Grabbing her recharged phone off the nightstand, she discovered multiple texts awaiting her. Frantic messages from MaryDru, Scott and at least a dozen from Victoria.

A message from MaryDru said, *I'm so, so sorry. I never meant to fall in love with Scott. Please don't hate me. Where are you, A.B.?*

She sucked in a breath. As if she could ever hate her beloved baby sister. And she knew MaryDru would've never set out to hurt her. Nor Scott, either.

AnnaBeth scrolled farther down the feed. Another one from Mary Dru. *Tell me you're okay. I'm so worried, A.B. Please call. Scott and I will never see one another again.*

Not at all what AnnaBeth wanted. MaryDru's happiness was why she'd run away in the first place.

She opened Scott's message.

Contrite, sincere Scott. Taking the blame for waiting so long to be honest with himself and her. Begging for her forgiveness. Promising to never see MaryDru again if AnnaBeth would just come home.

Sinking onto the pillow, she closed her eyes.

Scott had been a fixture in their lives. The son her father always wanted. Like a brother to her. She now suspected that had been the problem all along.

Yet when he'd looked at MaryDru at the church...

Perhaps no one would ever look at AnnaBeth that way, but she wouldn't stand by and allow MaryDru to miss her chance at true love.

Rolling onto her stomach, AnnaBeth texted Scott. *Nothing to forgive. I want you both to be happy. Don't give up on MaryDru. Tell her I'm safe and well.*

She hit Send. There. That would hopefully get them talking to each other again.

The chain of messages from Victoria mocked her. But without a fortifying cup of coffee, no way she was up to facing those. She turned off the phone.

With one glance at the bedside clock, she threw off the covers. After donning jeans and one of her favorite sweaters, she padded downstairs in her stockinged feet, eager to lend a hand, but she found Deirdre almost finished with breakfast preparations.

"Deirdre, I'm so sorry. I meant to help with breakfast, but I overslept."

Jonas's mother stirred the pot on the stove. "After yesterday, I'm sure you were completely wiped out." After setting the ladle on a ceramic spoon rest, she replaced the lid on the pot. "And not only physically."

AnnaBeth wrung her hands. "But I wanted to do something to repay you for your generosity."

Deirdre's gaze scanned her face. Her eyes were kind. "No need to repay us. It's our pleasure to have you here for as long as you need us."

AnnaBeth wasn't so sure. Despite Jonas's words last night, she seemed to get on his last nerve. Maybe if she could manage to stay out of his way as much as possible for the duration…

"I'm not so sure your son would agree with your open-ended hospitality, Deirdre."

"My son doesn't mean to come off so harsh." She glanced out the window that overlooked the barnyard. "As a child, Jonas was always my quiet little guy, but after what happened with Hunter's mother, he's become so withdrawn."

What *had* happened with Jonas's wife? She wouldn't dream of prying. Especially not with her own life in such disarray.

"It's not healthy for him or Hunter." Deirdre's chin trembled. "I'm afraid Jonas has lost the ability to trust, to hope. He tries to hide it, but underneath the gruffness, he's unhappy."

AnnaBeth's heart contracted. "I'm sorry."

His mother swiped her finger under her eye. "I

don't mean to unload on you like this, but you're very easy to talk to."

AnnaBeth nodded. "I get that a lot. I suppose I have the kind of face that invites confidences. And I promise I'd never breathe a word of what you've told me to anyone else."

"I sensed that about you immediately." She cupped AnnaBeth's cheek. "I think your ability to empathize is a rare gift. Your family must be so proud of you."

AnnaBeth's eyes moistened. "My family is complicated. And what happened yesterday will only make things worse." She blinked away the tears.

Deirdre squeezed her hand. "I'm sorry, honey, for what you went through yesterday. It must have been a painful blow losing your fiancé."

"It's not that." AnnaBeth fingered her earring. "You see, I never loved Scott."

Deirdre threw her a startled look. "You knew you didn't love him?"

She took a quick breath. "Jonas and Hunter are blessed to have you. You're also very easy to talk to."

If only her real mother hadn't died. If only Victoria had been like Deirdre Fielding, how different would her life had been?

Deirdre took off the lid and stirred the oatmeal on the stovetop. "Church has been canceled due to the snow. We'll have our own service here at the lodge." She stopped stirring. "But don't feel obligated to participate if that's not something you're interested in."

"I'd love to celebrate the Lord's Day with your family, Miss Deirdre."

Yet thinking about the uptown congregation which she'd fled from so ingloriously, she winced. Her father must have been livid at having to send home the wedding guests. Not to mention Victoria's undoubted complete mortification.

AnnaBeth desperately needed a distraction. "How about I set the table?"

"Thank you, honey. That would be a help." She opened a cabinet door and removed a set of porcelain bowls. "You know where to find the utensils."

"Breakfast for four?" Pulling out a drawer, AnnaBeth tried for a nonchalance she didn't feel. "Where is everyone?"

"Jonas is in the barn. And Hunter is getting in his roping practice on the terrace."

She stopped counting spoons. "Roping?"

Deirdre ladled the steaming oatmeal into a bowl. "At last year's championship, he won second place in his age division. He's determined to win first place in March."

She nudged the drawer shut with her hip. "There's a roping championship for four-year-olds?"

Deirdre set the bowl of oatmeal on the red-checked place mat. "There sure is."

After placing the spoons at each place setting, she began folding the napkins like Victoria had taught her. "He'll win a trophy, I guess?"

Deirdre returned to the table with another bowl. "Not a trophy. A silver rodeo belt buckle."

"For real?"

"Rodeo buckles mean bragging rights, even for a four-year-old." Deirdre transferred a container of blueberries into a pottery bowl. "Hunter is simply following in his dad's footsteps."

"I didn't realize Jonas was a rodeo champion."

She handed AnnaBeth the bowl to put on the table. "Not in roping, but before Hunter was born Jonas spent a few years on the rodeo circuit as a bronc buster."

"Wow." AnnaBeth blinked.

Jonas Stone was the real deal.

The back door creaked open.

"Bronc riding?" Glancing toward the door, AnnaBeth frowned. "Isn't that dangerous?"

Jonas leaned the lanky length of himself against the door frame. "Only if you fall off."

She blushed.

Deirdre spooned brown sugar into a small crystal bowl. "Somebody call Hunter to breakfast."

"I will." Moving toward the back door, she had to squeeze past Jonas. "Um… Excuse me…"

Stepping over his feet at the same moment he decided to retract them, she stumbled. Grabbing both her elbows, he caught her. And she found herself face-to-chest with the soft, green-checked flannel of his shirt.

AnnaBeth felt a tidal wave of crimson surge from the collar of her sweater up her neck. "Sorry to be so clumsy."

She risked a swift glance at his features.

His cheeks above the beard stubble flushed. "It's my fault. Shouldn't have taken up so much space."

Their eyes locked and held.

"No, it's—"

"Hello? Yoo-hoo…" An amused smile on her face, Deirdre tapped her shoe on the floor. "Call Hunter. Remember?"

Immediately, Jonas dropped his hold on AnnaBeth. "Right."

"Of course." Smoothing her hair, AnnaBeth stepped back. "I'm on it."

Throwing open the door, she closed her eyelids for a second, allowing the rush of air to cool her cheeks.

She heard the clatter of boots, and in a whoosh, small arms encircled her hips. Her eyes flew open.

"AnnaBef!" His face buried in her sweater, Hunter's voice was muffled. "I missed you."

She smiled. "While you were asleep, you missed me?"

Cowboy hat pushed to his hairline, Hunter lifted his head. "I'm so happy you're here wif me." He twined his little fingers into her hand.

Her heart skipped a beat. So, so sweet. "I'm happy to be here with you, too, Hunter." It was true.

Because of the sixth sense she always got around Jonas, even before he spoke, somehow she knew he was standing close behind her.

"Grandma has breakfast ready, Hunt. Time to come inside."

Hunter didn't let go of her hand. "Okay, Dad." He pulled her across the threshold with him.

The glower had returned to Jonas's face. "Wash your hands, please." He touched Hunter's shoulder.

Hunter gave AnnaBeth an endearing smile. "I'll be wight back, AnnaBef. Okay?"

"Okay," she whispered, disentangling her fingers from his.

She and Jonas watched him disappear into the lavatory off the mudroom.

Jonas sighed. "I've never seen him take to someone like he does you. But if he becomes a pest—"

"Hunter's wonderful." AnnaBeth opened her

hands. "Who wouldn't be proud to have such a sweet son like him?"

"You'd think so, wouldn't you?" Jonas ran his hand over his hair. "But not everyone..." His Adam's apple bobbing, he turned toward the kitchen.

She supposed some people might be annoyed by kids, but not her. She loved children.

Later, at the table, Jonas relayed what he'd learned about getting her car fixed. "Until the roads are cleared, I'm afraid you're stranded at the ranch."

"AnnaBeth wants to worship with us this morning, son."

Hunkered over his coffee, Jonas said nothing.

But the little cowboy perked in his booster seat. "I bee-weave in God. Do you, AnnaBef?"

A sudden silence fell over the table. Deirdre and Jonas exchanged glances.

"Not everyone is as comfortable talking about God as our family, Hunter." Deirdre touched his arm. "AnnaBeth may not want to—"

"It's okay." She lifted her gaze. "Yes, Hunter, I believe in God."

"Yay!" Hunter turned toward his father. "Bee-weaving is important, wight, Dad? If AnnaBef is going to be my—"

"Believing is important for everyone, Hunter." Cheeks reddening, Jonas dropped his gaze.

She wished her feelings about God could be as

simple as Hunter's childlike faith. She'd been only slightly older than him when her mother died. Her childhood had been lonely.

Coming to live with her father and his new wife, she'd felt alone most of the time. Always on the outside, especially with her dad, Hayes. And after yesterday, when she'd failed her father so badly…

She wondered if God still believed in her.

"Can I sit with AnnaBef while you wead, Dad?"

Jonas's eyes darted to her.

She smiled. "Of course he can."

Almost before she could finish speaking, Hunter scrambled out of his chair and hopped into her lap. Sighing, he nestled into her arms.

Scooting back his chair, Jonas ventured over to the built-in desk and returned carrying a small black bible. Sitting down again, Jonas began flipping pages. "Where were we last time?"

"Last time?" She arched an eyebrow. "Do you often become snowbound?"

"Thankfully, no." Deirdre laughed. "Our church is doing a read-through-the-bible program this year. And Jonas also does a devotional for interested guests on summer Sundays."

Hunter nodded. "I wuv cowboy Sundays."

Jonas continued to turn pages. "My stepdad built a small amphitheater behind the cabins overlooking the Blue Ridge."

AnnaBeth tilted her head. "I can't imagine a more wonderful setting. The glory of God's creation and God's Word celebrated by God's people."

Jonas looked up sharply. "That's how I've always felt, too."

"Today's the First Sunday of Advent." Deirdre motioned. "Why don't you do the reading from Isaiah 9, son?"

"What's Advent?" Hunter asked.

"It means coming." Jonas cleared his throat. "The First Sunday of Advent celebrates our hope."

AnnaBeth could sure use some hope after yesterday. Hunter leaned into her. She smiled. His hair smelled like baby shampoo.

Jonas read the passage from the bible.

"I wuv Chwistmas." Resting his head against her shoulder, Hunter scrutinized her face. "Do you wuv Chwistmas, AnnaBef?"

At the Cummings house, Christmas consisted of a never-ending, social merry-go-round. And impossible expectations of family perfection. Frayed nerves often led to arguments between her father and Victoria.

She gazed into Hunter's sweet face. "Maybe this year…"

Hunter grinned. "I know what we should do today."

Jonas raised his eyebrows. "I'm almost afraid to ask."

Deirdre shushed him. "What is it we ought to do today, Hunter?"

"We should decowate a Chwistmas tree today."

Deirdre looked at Jonas. "We usually decorate the house the weekend after Thanksgiving."

AnnaBeth straightened. "That sounds like fun. I'd love to help."

Jonas frowned. "I've attached the snowplow to the tractor. I'm going to try to clear a path to the main road, but we don't have our tree yet, Hunt. And we won't be able to get to town to buy one. Not today."

Hunter's face fell. "Can't we do something fun? It's a snow day, Dad."

"The ranch doesn't run itself." Jonas fingered the handle on his coffee cup. "Snow means I've just got more work to do."

His mother's lips pursed. "Work is all you ever do, Jonas."

Decorating the tree had sounded fun. And not just because of Hunter's Christmas joy. Yet what of her resolution to avoid Jonas? She should be glad he was too busy to hang around the house.

She stole a look at his rugged features. Perhaps he didn't want to hang around because of her. Trundling Hunter off her lap, she scraped back her chair to gather the dirty silverware.

Deirdre tried shooing her away. "You don't have to wash up."

"I like keeping busy." She reached for Jonas's empty bowl. "You cooked, Deirdre. It's only right that I clean. And then I'll get out of everyone's way, I promise."

"You're not in the way, AnnaBeth. My mom and Hunter are happy to have you with us." Jonas grabbed the other side of the bowl and held on. "And so am I."

Her being here made Jonas happy? *Don't read too much into what he said. He's just being polite.*

But she couldn't help feeling pleased. She smiled at him. Abruptly, he let go of the bowl.

Passing a hand over his face, he took a deep breath. "Maybe we can string popcorn tonight for when we have a tree to decorate. How would that be?"

Hunter bounced in his boots. "Hoo-way!"

And though his words had undoubtedly been meant for his son, she couldn't help noticing that his gaze remained fixed.

On her.

Chapter Five

Ensconced in what had become her favorite chair in the lodge, AnnaBeth spent the next hour with her laptop working on her blog.

For the last half hour, Hunter had zoomed a miniature green tractor around the braided rug at her feet. Pausing his rumbling engine noises, he popped his head above the arm of the chair. "Can we go pway outside, AnnaBef?"

Gazing out the window at the frosty landscape, she would just as soon sit by the well-stoked fire and drink hot chocolate. But one look at his wistful brown eyes, and she surged to her feet.

"That sounds like a great idea."

Hunter fist-pumped the air. "Yay!"

Deirdre strolled into the living room. "What's with all the commotion?"

"AnnaBef and I awe going outside to pway,

Gwam-ma." His eyes shone. "She's de best Chwistmas pwesent ever."

She cut her eyes at his grandmother. "What?"

"Uh… Get your hat and coat, Hunt. And your boots."

Was it AnnaBeth's imagination, or had Deirdre deliberately ignored her question?

Hunter raced toward the mudroom.

"Not your cowboy boots," Deirdre called after him. "Your snow boots." She turned toward AnnaBeth. "Thank you for taking him outside. Having to stay cooped up indoors is hard on him. His father was the same way."

Both women cringed at the sound of a dull thud.

"Sowee, Gwam-ma!"

They exchanged amused glances.

"I'd take him out myself, but this cold…" Deirdre put a hand across her chest. "Every year, winter feels colder to my joints."

AnnaBeth tucked her phone into her pocket. "I don't mind. Truly I don't. I love spending time with Hunter."

"That's so sweet of you to say."

"I mean it."

His grandmother smiled. "I know you do. You'll make a wonderful mother one day."

She flushed. "Thank you. Hunter is very easy to love. But after yesterday's fiasco, motherhood isn't something even remotely on my horizon."

"The thing about horizons? Sometimes you only need to look up." Deirdre gestured toward the mountain ridge, visible through the window-pane. "As the day progresses, the view only gets better... Oh, no."

AnnaBeth stiffened. "What is it?"

Hunter's grandmother put her hand to her mouth. "Please tell me you weren't planning a honeymoon to the Bahamas. Do you have any winter clothing in your suitcase?"

"I do." She nodded. "We were going to Aspen. I don't ski, but Scott is an avid skier."

"Scott?" Jonas growled.

At his voice, she angled.

Standing next to the long dining-room table, his lips twisted. "Your fiancé's name is Scott?"

"Was." She blinked. "I mean, of course, his name is still Scott." Why did she always get so flustered with Jonas Stone? "Scott isn't my fiancé anymore." She sighed. "But you know that."

"So let me get this straight. You don't ski, but you were going to spend your honeymoon on the slopes because your ex-fiancé liked to ski." Jonas's brown eyes darkened. "Why didn't this Scott person choose a place you'd both enjoy?"

"I didn't mind. Truly." She shrugged. "I was going to catch up on my reading. Work on future blog posts. That sort of thing."

Jonas glared at her. "While your ex-fiancé

was out enjoying himself? Leaving you alone on your honeymoon?"

Put that way, he made her sound like a perfect idiot. Not a news flash. Only an idiot got herself stranded on a mountain in the middle of a snowstorm in a wedding dress.

She was further irritated—at herself—that his opinion mattered so much.

"AnnaBef!" Hunter shouted from the mudroom.

"Coming," she called. Moving to the stairs, she gave Jonas and his mother a small smile.

"I'll just go get my boots and coat."

Jonas watched her climb the stairs.

His mother pursed her lips. "Must you bark at her, son?"

Jonas scrubbed his hand over his face. "I didn't mean to sound so gruff. But what kind of groom…?" He gritted his teeth.

His mother patted his shoulder. "The same kind who would leave AnnaBeth at the altar." She glanced at the staircase. "Although, I get the feeling there's more to that story than she's said."

Jonas lifted his hat and combed his fingers through his hair. "It makes me crazy to see her allow someone to run roughshod over her feelings."

"She's a people-pleaser, Jonas. You retreat. And she goes out of her way to appease." His mother flicked her eyes at him. "Seems to me a healthier response lies somewhere in the middle."

Resettling his hat, he decided to ignore her last remark. "AnnaBeth is going to have to toughen up, or she isn't going to make it in the cold, cruel world." Scowling, he rubbed the back of his neck, working out the kinks with his hand. "She's not our responsibility, Mom. Don't get too attached."

"Why do I feel you're really talking to yourself?" His mother quirked an eyebrow at him. "There's an old saying that once you save a person's life, you remain forever connected to them."

His heart seized. Connected to AnnaBeth Cummings for life?

"Was there something you needed, Jonas?"

He blinked at his mother.

"The reason you came back inside the house?"

"I—I…"

Why *had* he come inside the house? *Oh, yeah. To see what AnnaBeth was doing.*

Jonas scowled. "I was going to call Zach again. Get an update on the snow plows's progress."

His mother folded her arms. "Do tell why you're so anxious to be rid of our houseguest, son."

Jonas rocked back. "Once Zach fixes her car, she can be someone else's problem."

His mother's lips tightened. "Jonas…"

At a sudden creak, he glanced up at the landing and discovered AnnaBeth staring down at them.

She wore a pink puffy ski jacket, a dark pink knit cap and matching scarf. From the forward thrust of her chin, he suspected she'd heard every word he said.

Face-to-face with AnnaBeth Cummings in all her perky winter glory, he fled to the refuge of the barn. Where he buried himself in a flurry of work. Mucking out the horse stalls. Stacking bales on the flatbed trailer behind the hay barn.

He'd make a trip out to the far pasture to feed the horses this afternoon. Hunter liked feeding the herd. His son's laughter floated into the barn. Venturing around the corner, he gazed out at a scene that caused his heart to catch.

Romping through the snow, Hunter tossed a snowball at AnnaBeth. Squealing, she ducked a fraction too late. Hunter had a pretty good arm for a preschooler. For such a little guy, he could be laser-focused when he had a goal. Not unlike his father.

Although, Jonas's days on the rodeo circuit were best forgotten. He'd fallen away from his faith and gotten involved with Kasey. Neither of which had turned out well for him.

His son's laughter rippled across the distance, even after AnnaBeth pelted him with a snowball of her own. Despite his failed marriage, Jonas would go through the pain all over again if it meant having his son in his life.

Jonas needed to apologize to AnnaBeth. It wasn't like him to be rude. But something about the woman…

Pushing off from the barn, he headed toward his son and the flatlander.

"Dad!" Hunter yelled, catching sight of him. "I taught AnnaBeth how to make snow angels. Can you bee-weave she's never made snow angels?"

She dropped her eyes to her expensive leather boots. "Winter storms usually only bring ice to Charlotte."

"Not so good for snow angels," he rasped.

She looked at him. "No. Not so good for snow angels."

He held her gaze. "But I'm sure Charlotte offers charms of its own."

Pink flooded her cheeks. "If you say so."

Energy on wheels, his son giddy-upped around them as if on an imaginary horse.

"I hope you'll forgive me for what I said earlier." He stuffed his hands in his pockets. "I didn't mean for it to come out the way it sounded."

"Dad, let's make snow angels." Hunter jumped up and down. "You, too."

He pushed up the brim of his hat. "Uh… I don't know, Hunter. It's been a long time since I had time to make snow angels."

"AnnaBef and I can teach you, can't we, AnnaBef?" He touched his father's coat sleeve. "Pwease? It's easy."

"Okay." No longer able to resist joining in the fun, Jonas smiled at his son's upturned face. "What do I do first?"

"Sit down in de snow. Wike dis." Hunter plopped his bottom onto the ground. "Show him."

Crouching slightly, she fell backward onto her backside. "Your turn, Jonas…"

After depositing his hat onto a nearby stump, he eased onto the snow between her and his son. "Now what?"

Hunter waved his hand as if guiding a reversing pickup. "Awe de way, Dad…"

Stretching out flat on his back, Jonas found himself gazing at the picture-perfect blue sky.

"Move your awms and wegs, Dad."

Just to be silly, he raised his arms and legs straight up in the air and flapped them.

AnnaBeth laughed. He almost smiled before he caught himself.

"No, Dad. Wike dis. Jumping jacks in the snow. Watch me."

Hunter proceeded to sweep the snow with his small limbs.

She smiled. "You're the best snow-angel maker I've ever seen, Hunter."

Hunter's chin bobbed. "I'm also good at building snowmen. And woping. And…"

AnnaBeth turned her head toward Jonas. "I love his confidence. You've done a great job raising him."

Something long numb inside Jonas's heart warmed. "Thank you. It hasn't been easy, but God never failed me."

God had provided everything they'd needed—a strong support network with his mom, friends and, yes, even the pesky Truelove troublemakers. Everything they needed, except a wife and a mother.

Gazing into the deep green of AnnaBeth's eyes, he couldn't help but wonder if God might intend more for him and Hunter this Christmas than he'd ever imagined possible.

His heart leaped in his chest.

All because of a runaway bride who somehow ran into their path one snowy night.

Lying beside her in the snow, Jonas's dark eyes grew distant. AnnaBeth wasn't sure why.

He'd seemed so happy a moment ago. But it was like he didn't believe he deserved to be happy. And so, emotionally, he'd just shut down.

"Dad!" Hunter jumped up from the snow. "Dad, you're not making a snow angel."

Jonas jolted, as if returning from a place or time long distant. Maybe from whatever happened between him and Hunter's mom.

Since childhood, AnnaBeth had believed it was her job to make sure everyone was happy. So she felt compelled to bring Jonas back to the joy of the moment. To Hunter. To her.

Not to you, AnnaBeth. Don't be stupid.

She cleared her throat. "Hunter and I found it enormously helpful in the creative process of snow-angel making to sing."

Jonas turned his face to her. "Creative process of snow-angel making…" His lips quirked. "Such a natural gift with words. No wonder you write that blog thing."

She rolled her eyes, as he'd no doubt meant her to, but she now had his attention. "Sing, Jonas."

A slight crease puckered his forehead. "You want me to sing?" He nearly smiled.

"You're a cowboy. So sing."

Another near miss on that smile of his… So close but almost only counted with horseshoes. Not with handsome cowboys.

"What do you want me to sing?"

Hunter loomed over them. "It's Chwistmas. Sing 'Jingle Bells,' ev-wee-body."

"Good idea." Her lips parted. "'Jingle bells, jingle bells, jingle—'" She jabbed his bicep. "You're not singing, Jonas."

"Yeah, Dad." Hunter planted his fists on his jeans. "You're not singing."

A corner of Jonas's mouth tugged upward. "But I don't sing."

Not a full-blown smile, but it was progress.

"Why not?" She rested her cheek against the snow.

"Trust me, it's better this way. Your ears wouldn't appreciate my efforts."

"You let me be the judge of that, Jonas Stone. You *have* to sing. For the best results, you must enter into the spirit of snow-angel making."

"Fine." He blew out a breath. "But don't say I didn't warn you."

"Oh, and at the same time you're singing, Jonas, don't forget to do those jumping jacks with your arms and legs in the snow. Got it?"

"Got it." He took a lungful of clean mountain air. "Jingle bells…"

She smiled. Now they were getting somewhere. "Jingle bells, jingle all the way…"

"Oh what fun," Hunter interjected.

She laughed.

"It is to sing—" wind-milling his arms and legs, Jonas joined him "—on a one-horse. Open. Sleigh." They finished with a flourish.

Hunter clapped his mittens together. "Dat was awesome, Dad."

Jonas stuck his tongue in his cheek. "I told you it would be bad, AnnaBeth."

"You have a nice voice. A bit rusty but nothing a little exercise wouldn't cure."

"Says the woman who gives her voice a fair amount of exercise." But he smiled as he said it, taking the sting out of his words.

AnnaBeth fluttered her lashes at him. "True."

"What's next?" he asked.

"Here's the tricky part. Getting up without ruining your masterpiece." Pushing upright, she propelled herself onto her feet. And offered him her hand.

Sitting up, he took hold of her gloved hand. Bracing herself, with her boots slightly apart, she pulled him to his feet.

"And there you are." She drew his attention to the imprint he'd left behind in the snow. "A beautiful Christmas angel."

Hunter inserted his small self between their bodies. "Dad's awe handsome." He hugged her leg. "AnnaBefs awe boo-ti-full."

Leaning, she planted a quick kiss on his red knit cap. "You keep saying things like that, and you'll never get rid of me, Hunter."

He hung onto her arm. "I never want you to weave, AnnaBef. I want you to stay wif me fo-wever."

Jonas's brow creased. "AnnaBeth has her own life, Hunt. She has her own family. Her own friends."

Hunter shook his head. "We can be her fami-wee, Dad. You can be AnnaBef's fwend. Wight?"

Jonas gave his son a halfhearted shrug. "Sure. You, Gramma, me. We can all be friends with AnnaBeth."

Except she felt anything but friendliness coming from him. Moments earlier, he'd appeared to be having such a good time with them.

Perhaps only a good time with his son. Her heart pricked. Why didn't Jonas like her? Most people liked her. People loved having her as a friend.

Friend, yes. As a girlfriend? Not so much.

Hunter tugged her hand. Though his father was determined to keep her at arm's length, at least the little cowboy liked her. "I want to wope my steer."

Jonas retrieved his hat. "The driveway's not going to clear itself. I'd better get back to it."

He walked away toward the barn, and she told herself it didn't matter. Give or take another few days at most, Jonas would never have to bother speaking to her again.

All for the best. The FieldStone was his world. And hers? To Be Determined.

It shouldn't matter so much that he didn't want to be her friend. She watched the broad outline of his shoulders until he disappeared into the barn.

Shouldn't matter. But somehow it did.

Chapter Six

After promising to create snow people later, AnnaBeth finally convinced Hunter to come inside the house to eat lunch.

"Slow down, Hunter. You don't have to inhale it all in one gulp." Deirdre set a bowl of vegetable soup in front of AnnaBeth at the kitchen table. "And you've been a trouper hanging out in the freezing cold with Hunter all morning."

AnnaBeth liked the sunny kitchen at the lodge. The stainless-steel appliances of the commercial kitchen were coupled with weathered white cabinets. Yet the red-checkered curtains and the rooster-topped island gave off a warm, inviting feel. Even style-maven Victoria would've approved.

Hunter paused between slurps. "We're going to make snow people next, Gwam-ma."

In a rush of cold air, Jonas came inside the

house. "Don't you think you ought to give AnnaBeth a chance to dethaw before you go outside again, Hunt?" After shedding his coat and gloves, he toed out of his work boots, leaving them at the door. "Maybe she has things to do this afternoon."

He hung his coat on the peg, then padded into the kitchen. The socks were identical to the socks Hunter had given her to wear last night. And the socks gave her an idea for a post and photo.

Thinking she'd be on her honeymoon, AnnaBeth had prescheduled this week's posts, but it never hurt to get ahead.

"Don't feel obligated to entertain my energetic son, AnnaBeth." Pulling out a chair at the farm table, Jonas touched his son's shoulder. "AnnaBeth is not your personal playmate, Hunt."

Hunter thrust out his small jaw. "I know she's not, Dad. 'Cause AnnaBef is my—"

"We talked about this, Hunter."

Her eyes darted from father to son. She was missing something here. An unspoken conversation to which she wasn't privy. She reminded herself to mind her own business.

Deirdre placed a bowl in front of Jonas and then turned away, coughing into her arm.

"Mom?" He frowned. "The cold sounds like it's settled in your lungs."

Deirdre waved her hand. "You know how it is this time of year with the fluctuating temperatures." She smiled. "Last week was almost balmy. This week, snow."

AnnaBeth dipped her spoon into the soup. "Welcome to North Carolina."

His handsome lips curved. "Because if you don't like the weather…"

She laughed. "Give it a day and it's likely to change."

Jonas's gaze caught hers and held. So, so handsome and, even better, such a wonderful father and son.

It seemed to AnnaBeth that they stared at each other a long time, but it was probably only the space of a heartbeat. Yet long enough to send her heart into a stutter step. Hunter's spoon clattering against his bowl broke the moment.

Cheeks ruddy from the outdoors, Jonas bent over his soup. Flushing, AnnaBeth concentrated on spooning the nourishing broth into her mouth.

"You're taking something for your cough, right, Mom?"

"I'm actually running low on over-the-counter meds." Deirdre wiped the granite countertop. "I meant to pick up something at the drugstore, but forgot."

Jonas rested his forearms on the table. "If preschool isn't canceled tomorrow, I'll get some for you when I drop off Hunter."

"Thanks, hon." She winked at AnnaBeth.

"Stranded by the snow, I guess for now we'll have to make the most of our snow holiday."

"Yay!" Hunter fist-pumped the air. "AnnaBef and I are going to build the world's gweatest snow people."

Jonas raised an eyebrow. "Hunt…"

"Sowee, Dad." Hunter lifted his head. "What would you like to do next with me, AnnaBef?"

AnnaBeth hid her smile.

"Not exactly what I meant." Jonas shook his head. "Maybe she wants to go to her room and take a nap, Hunt. Alone."

"Oh." His big brown eyes drooped. "I'm sowee, AnnaBef."

Getting up, she came around the table and gave him a hug. "I would love to make snow people with you, sweetie pie, but let's stay inside and warm up first. I have an idea how you could help me work on my blog, though."

"I can help." Hunter squared his shoulders. "I'm big."

AnnaBeth kissed the top of his head. "You are very big. So big. The best, biggest boy ever."

Soon after, Jonas brought his bowl to the sink and left once more to work on clearing the drive. And with the unflagging energy only children possessed, Hunter decided to head to the terrace to practice his roping again.

"I'll teach you how to wope a steer, too. Just a few minutes... Pwease, AnnaBef?"

Who could resist those chocolate-brown eyes? Not her. And why shouldn't she take advantage of a free roping lesson?

Never could tell when knowing how to rope a steer might come in handy in metropolitan Charlotte.

"I'll come in a few minutes. After I wash the dishes for your gramma." She turned on the sink faucet. "Are you feeling okay, Deirdre?"

The already trim woman had eaten practically nothing for lunch.

"I'll watch Hunter for a few hours if you'd like to get some rest." Thinking she might have overstepped boundaries, she said, "If you feel okay about entrusting him into my care, that is."

Deirdre gave her a genuine smile. "You may be the most trustworthy young lady I've ever had the privilege to meet." She sighed. "To tell the truth, my get-up-and-go appears to have got up and went. I'd love the chance to catch a quick nap, if you don't mind watching Hunter."

"Mind? I can't think of anything more fun than spending time with him."

Deirdre's face lit up as if AnnaBeth had provided an answer to a question she hadn't asked. "Hunter loves spending time with you. Already you have a special place in his heart."

"And he in mine, Deirdre."

Moisture welled in Deirdre's brown eyes. "I've prayed so often about Hunter and Jonas's situation. But I believe God may be about to do more than I could ever dare dream…"

Unsure what she meant, AnnaBeth nodded, anyway. "God is like that, isn't He?"

"Yes, He is." Deirdre fanned her flushed face. "Forgive me. I'm not usually so emotional." Spots of color mottled Deirdre's fair complexion.

AnnaBeth squirted detergent into the dishwater. "You're not feeling yourself. And then, of course, we always have to factor in our hair." Hands wet, she used her shoulder to swipe a strand of hair out of her eyes.

Deirdre's mouth quirked. "You have lovely hair. The color makes us unique. And passionate about those we love. But you might be right." She wagged a finger. "Sensible folk know better than to mess with a redhead."

"Our hair is like a public service announcement." AnnaBeth smirked. "An emergency-alert warning system—'Redhead Coming. Beware!'"

Laughing, Deirdre cocked her head. "A rancher's wife has to be tough, that's for sure, but I'm starting to think maybe it's time to bestow that mantle on someone else." The landline rang, and Deirdre excused herself. "Dwight?"

Whoever Dwight was—he'd called Deirdre

yesterday, too. Did Jonas's mother have a budding romance of her own?

Perhaps last night's remark about the inn on the Eastern Shore of Virginia had been more about Deirdre's personal interest than pointed at anyone else.

AnnaBeth wondered if Jonas was aware of what was going on with his mother.

Not your business, AnnaBeth. Stay in your own lane. Stop being so nosy.

After finishing the dishes, she spread the drying cloth over the drain board. She shrugged into her coat and joined Hunter on the terrace.

On the far end of the long terrace sat a green plastic steer. Hunter showed her how to fold over the rope about an arm's length to coil it. He taught her the proper way to hold the rope—her index finger pointed on the shank of the rope toward the knotted part Hunter called the hondo.

He swung the rope in a circle above his head. "Keep your finger on de wope pointed at de tawget."

She watched his technique closely. His rotating wrist kept the rope smooth and open. He tossed the rope toward the dummy horns.

Like a pitcher's arm followed through with a baseball, Hunter's arm followed the toss. The rope landed as intended, the loop falling around the steer head. Then, reaching, he jerked the rope and pulled the knot tight.

She clapped. "Hooray!"

Accomplishment shining in his face, he grinned. "Now you, AnnBef."

Her wrist action wasn't as smooth. She had a hard time not lassoing herself and becoming entangled in the rope. Try after try, she fell short, the rope landing on the plastic steer's rump and not around his neck.

"Don't be sad, AnnaBef. I've been pwacticing a wong, wong time. Since I was a wittle kid."

She tapped the brim of his cowboy hat. "Since then, huh?"

After the brisk arm exercise, she began feeling soreness in muscles she never knew she possessed. So she convinced Hunter to come inside for a hot-chocolate break.

Later, Hunter helped her set up some shots for an impromptu photo shoot. Then she and Hunter took a lot of silly selfies.

With Deirdre still resting, they decided to find a book to quietly read together.

Finger to his lips, Hunter beckoned AnnaBeth to follow him upstairs. They crept past Deirdre's closed bedroom.

Hunter gestured toward a half-open door. "Dat's my dad's room."

She didn't want to violate Jonas's privacy so

she didn't venture inside, but she got a glimpse of the stark bedroom. Victoria believed a bedroom should reflect the occupant's personality, but there was nothing there of Jonas. And that bothered AnnaBeth.

Did Jonas feel as forlorn as the room appeared? *Not your business, AnnaBeth. Not your bedroom. Not your problem how Jonas feels or does not feel.*

Hunter's bedroom was next to his father's. And when she stepped inside, she smiled. As it should, the room reflected the little boy's personality.

Wall posters depicted cowboys roping steers. A toy box overflowed with dinosaurs, Matchbox cars and a segmented race-car track. The twin bed was covered with a colorful red-and-blue cowboy-themed comforter.

Hunter motioned to the framed photograph on top of a small pine bookcase. "Dat's my mudder, Kasey. But I don't 'member her."

The forever twentysomething woman wore a blue, Western-cut shirt with pearl snaps. Her long, curly blond hair waved from under a black Stetson.

Jonas's wife hadn't just been pretty. She'd been gorgeous.

The picture was an action shot in the middle of an arena. Atop a powerful black horse, Kasey Stone gripped the reins. At what appeared breakneck speed, hunched over the horse, Hunter's mother rounded a barrel. Her blue eyes were narrowed. Her face intent. An accomplished horsewoman.

As for AnnaBeth's skill set?

She wrote silly little words about frivolous, pretty things for people to buy. She could decorate a room like nobody's business. She knew clothes like Hunter knew roping.

AnnaBeth let out a sigh. And that, ladies and gentlemen, was about the extent of it.

Hunter pulled a book off the shelf. "Dis is one of my favowite books. About a wittle boy wike me named Peter." He handed it to her.

She examined the cover. "*The Snowy Day* sounds like the perfect book to read today."

Like a couple of cat burglars, they tiptoed downstairs to the chair in front of the fireplace. Only a few, glowing embers remained. When night fell, Jonas would probably get the fire blazing again.

She settled against the leather cushion. "I love this spot."

Book clasped to his chest, Hunter climbed into her lap. "I wuv you, AnnaBef."

She hugged the little boy close. "I love you, too, Hunter." And she realized it was true. He was so easy to love.

As for his father?

Jonas wasn't just hunky. His strong faith, his relationship with his child, his integrity... Jonas Stone was the real deal. In every possible way.

She could so easily lose her heart to Jonas and everything that was his life here at the FieldStone, but AnnaBeth and rejection were old acquaintances.

Don't be an idiot, AnnaBeth. Are you a glutton for punishment or what? Single doesn't mean available.

It was obvious Jonas had never gotten over the woman in the photograph upstairs. Probably would never get over her.

She opened the first page of the classic story of Peter's snowy day adventure.

"Is it as pwetty where you wive, AnnaBef, as de FieldStone?"

"It's pretty." She tapped her finger on the end of his nose. "But not as pretty as here."

"Good." Hunter pursed his lips. "'Cause you need to stay where it's de pwettiest." Tucking his head under her chin, he snuggled in her arms. "Wif me."

By the time she read "the end," Hunter had grown still. His breathing was soft. Very unlike her perpetually in-motion little cowboy.

Hers? Where had that come from? Nothing and no one here belongs to you, AnnaBeth. Nor you to them.

And most likely, never would.

Leaning over him, she saw that his eyelids were closed. She put aside the book and held him closer. It wasn't often she got the chance to hold a little one.

All too soon her own snowy day adventure would end. In all likelihood, she'd never see Hunter, Deirdre or Jonas again.

The realization made her inexplicably sad. But that was life. Her life, anyway.

Always full of goodbyes. First, her mom. Even after she came to live with her dad's new family, he always seemed to be saying goodbye. Jetting off on yet another business trip. She used to wish it was Victoria who left on the airplanes and not him.

She yawned. Hunter wasn't the only one worn out by the day's adventures. Or the only one needing a nap.

Deirdre was right. A rancher's wife had to be tough. Yet being Victoria's stepdaughter meant she'd had to be tough in her own way, too.

Speaking of her stepmother, she still hadn't opened Victoria's messages. She really ought to read them. AnnaBeth yawned again.

Maybe in a few minutes. Soon as she rested her eyes...

When Jonas ventured back into the lodge to take a break from the cold, he found the house unusually quiet.

In search of his family, his heart did a flip-flop at the sight of AnnaBeth and Hunter, sound asleep and nestled in the leather armchair. A children's book sat on the side table. Her arms curled protectively around him, his son had folded himself into her in a way Jonas hadn't seen him do since Hunter was a baby.

His eyes misted. Grandmas were wonderful, but there was nothing like a mother's love. And for the first time since Kasey died, he contemplated dating again.

For Hunter's sake, of course. To find the mother his son so desperately craved. But despite all the wishing in the world, it was not going to happen by Christmas.

When and if Jonas did seek a mother for Hunter, it would most certainly not be the very temporary AnnaBeth. But it gave Jonas something to think about, to plan for—for next year. An early New Year's resolution.

Jonas rubbed the stubble on his jawline.

Sure, he got lonely, but he was done with emotion. Who needed love? Hunter's needs were the only thing that mattered.

Feeling pretty good about his decision, it was then he noticed a tendril of wavy, red hair lying against AnnaBeth's cheek. And his mouth went dry.

The sweetness of seeing AnnaBeth with his

son caused an almost physical ache in the center of his chest.

He could have stood there for hours watching the both of them, but his eyes started to well up at how perfect they looked together. Thinking he could make a quiet retreat, he took one step backward when the pine board beneath his foot creaked.

AnnaBeth's eyes flew open.

Sorry, he mouthed.

Wait, she mouthed back.

Slowly, gently, she disentangled herself from Hunter's limbs. She inched her way out of the chair and tiptoed across the braided rug. She picked her camera off the dining-room table.

"Let him sleep," she whispered.

Jonas followed her into the kitchen. "Congratulations on wearing my son out. That may be a first."

She smoothed her hair out of her face. "He wore me out, too." She smirked.

He smiled. "What have you two been doing since lunch? And where's Mom?"

"Your mom decided to take a nap, so I convinced Hunter to have some quiet time with a book. And then we fell asleep, too. But not before we did this—" She clicked through the photos on her camera. "Hunter helped me set up the shot."

It was a photo of his wool socks on what he presumed to be AnnaBeth's feet, hanging over the arm of the chair. The glowing embers of the fire provided a cozy backdrop.

He gave her a sideways glance. "You took a picture of the socks?"

"I told you I loved those socks. My post will be a product endorsement. Readers will buy these like hotcakes."

"So you're saying I should buy sock stock while the price is still low?"

"Might not be a bad idea." She laughed. "No harm in diversifying."

"Diversifying? What did you do before you took up blogging? Investment banking?"

She frowned. "Actually, my father's in banking. He isn't around much. Always working, but I guess I couldn't help but pick up some of the lingo."

Jonas poured himself a cup of coffee from the carafe his mother kept warm all day this time of year. "I took a look at your blog this afternoon."

Her lashes swept upward across her cheeks. "You did?"

From the expression on her face, he could tell she wanted to ask him what he thought, but uncertainty held her back.

"You looked me up?" She went pink. "I mean, you looked up my blog."

He'd been interested. Intrigued. And unable

to stop himself from typing her name into the search engine.

"It's well-written, and the photos are well-done. You have an eye for color. Of course, it's also very girly."

"But so are my readers." She fluttered her lashes at him. "And in case you haven't noticed, so am I."

Oh, he'd noticed.

Jonas cocked his head. "Your posts have a witty touch. Although, knowing you, that doesn't surprise me a bit."

Witty, but sometimes too self-deprecating to his liking. He had a feeling AnnaBeth Cummings didn't give herself enough credit. He'd been wowed by her creativity and professionalism.

Skimming over several year's worth of posts, he'd run across photos of her family. The petite younger sister. The equally tiny and elegant stepmother.

Even one of AnnaBeth with some frat-looking dude—the evil ex-fiancé himself. No photos of home or her father, however.

A picture was starting to form in his mind of AnnaBeth's world before their lives intersected. Though lately, his life before meeting AnnaBeth felt hazier and hazier...

He ran the tip of his finger around the rim of his mug. "You do photo shoots all over the place."

She smiled. "I love to travel."

Whereas he never wanted to live anywhere but the ranch. "The blog's called *Heart's Home*, but you travel so much. Don't you ever miss home?"

Her smile faded. And the brittle, haughty air she appeared to be able to don at will fell between them.

Debutante AnnaBeth Cummings. So unlike the warm woman who cuddled his son and made snow angels, and whose nearness accelerated his heartbeat.

"Will Hunter be okay if I leave him in the chair?" She lifted her chin. "Or should I stay close?"

Sipping his coffee, Jonas leaned against the counter. "He'll be fine. Ranch kids are raised to entertain themselves. And when he wakes up, he knows to start on his chores."

AnnaBeth cocked her head. "He's four."

Jonas shrugged. "Age-appropriate chores, but ranch kids learn to pull their weight. They take pride in their contribution to the family business." Thinking of the upscale world from which she came, he frowned. "Probably sounds like child labor to you."

"Not at all. It makes sense," she said.

"From an early age, ranch kids learn their worth. Working alongside each other, they understand how valuable they are to their family."

Her mouth thinned. "Something every child should experience."

Jonas got the impression she didn't feel very valued or worthwhile to her family. Feelings reinforced by her no-good fiancé.

He sensed hidden hurts in AnnaBeth. So many painful wounds. And the extent of his wish to reassure her—to comfort her—shocked him.

"What have you been doing since lunch, Jonas?"

Momentarily robbed of speech, he stared at her. *Get it together, man. What's wrong with you? Getting mushy, just because of a pretty flatlander.*

She touched her hand to her cheek. "Did I drool while I was asleep? Is there something wrong with my face?"

His heart clamored. There was absolutely nothing wrong with her face.

And that was part of the problem. She wasn't just some pretty face. AnnaBeth was more. So much more than he ever imagined.

"Uh…" He took a deep, steadying breath. "I've been loading the hay wagon for the afternoon feed."

Her eyes lit. "You're going to feed the horses?"

Jonas looked at her over the rim of the mug. "Yes."

"Could I help?" she asked in a rush of words as if she feared he'd refuse. "Your mom has dinner going in the Crock-Pot. And I'm not used to being so idle."

He could see that about her. More energy than a pup. She and Hunter had that in common.

She tucked a tendril of hair behind her ear. "I like to keep busy."

Jonas liked to keep busy, too. There was no shortage of work to be done on a ranch. He drove himself hard every day until he practically fell into bed each night.

Hard work was the best remedy for keeping the regrets and what-ifs at bay. Keeping himself too tired to be lonely. Although last night, he'd lain awake a long time pondering their unexpected guest.

She twirled the strand of hair around her finger. "If you wouldn't mind the company, I'd love to help you, Jonas."

AnnaBeth had beautiful hair. Pulse-zinging, knee-buckling, gorgeous hair.

Jonas swallowed past the boulder lodged in his throat. "I—I wouldn't mind some company."

Her company in particular. He realized how silent his world had become. How barren and devoid of life.

Next year, Hunter would be going to kindergarten every day. And Jonas feared the silence might grow deafening.

For all her bright chatter, he liked spending

time with the flatlander. Being with AnnaBeth was like getting a dose of sunshine. And happiness, too. Outside of his son, it was something he hadn't experienced in a long time.

He felt an unusual connection with AnnaBeth that he hadn't known with anyone else since... Since never?

Jonas turned on the faucet and rinsed out the cup. "Won't take long with the two of us working together."

She blew out a breath. As if she'd feared he would turn her away. Like he had it in him to deny himself the opportunity to bask in her perennial cheerfulness.

Throwing him a big smile, she moved toward the mudroom to grab her coat. "I can't wait to start."

And suddenly, neither could he.

Chapter Seven

Her breath visible in the chilly afternoon air, AnnaBeth held the horse's bridle while Jonas harnessed Culpepper to the flatbed wagon loaded with hay.

"I'll need you to open the pasture gate and when I'm through, close it behind me."

Tossing his mane, Culpepper whinnied.

Eyebrow quirking, Jonas glanced at her over the Culpepper's broad, russet-colored back. "Was that a yes?"

"A yes from both of us." She stroked Culpepper's silky smooth nose. "What's the other horse's name?"

"Finian." Jonas stepped into the wagon. "You can climb aboard now." Reaching, he offered her his hand.

His hand was warm. Strong. Wonderful. She loved his hands.

Biting off a sigh, she allowed him to help her into the wagon. With the flatbed piled high with hay bales, it was standing-room-only at the front.

Making a clicking sound with his tongue against his teeth, he set the horses in motion. The wagon lurched. She fell against the rail.

"Whoa there." Jonas steadied her. "I probably should've mentioned it'll be a bumpy ride."

"No worries." She shrugged. "Just got to find my sea legs… I mean, wagon legs."

The wheels rolled over the snow toward the far line of the fence.

From under the brim of his cowboy hat, he cut his eyes at her. "Hang on to my arm."

Jonas's wish was her command. She placed her hand on the soft suede of his coat.

When they arrived at the pasture gate, she jumped down to unfasten the latch on the gate. Her boots crunched across the snow. Once he'd driven the team through, she swung the gate closed and refastened the catch.

A few yards ahead, he pulled the team to a stop, waiting for her. And once again, he leaned down to assist her into the wagon.

"Thanks," she whispered.

Only the snapping of the leather bridle and the wind sloughing through the snow-laden evergreens broke the companionable silence between them. There was a pine-scented tang in the air. Breathing deeply, she didn't feel the need for words. A first for her.

Within a few moments, however, she detected the sound of galloping hooves. About a dozen horses appeared at the top of the next ridge.

"They're beautiful." She let go of his arm. "The FieldStone Ranch is so beautiful. The air so pure and clean. I imagine your guests never want to leave."

His gaze raked her face. "I rode the rodeo circuit for a while, but once Hunter was born I've never wanted to live anywhere else."

"Hunter is very blessed to be able to call this place home."

A smile graced his cheeks. "I've always thought so. I'm glad you think so, too."

She gazed at the milling horses. "What do you want me to do now, Jonas?"

He steered the wagon in a half circle in the middle of the field. "You seem pretty comfortable around horses."

"Like many preteen girls, I was fairly horse-crazy." She smiled. "I guess some things never change."

"You've spent time with horses then?"

It always embarrassed AnnaBeth to talk about her silver-spoon childhood. Often, people made erroneous assumptions about her because of her father's wealth. And over the years, she learned to downplay that aspect of her life.

"My stepmother, Victoria, is horse-crazy, too. MaryDru and I have ridden since we were children." She lifted her chin. "I'm aware what people think about someone like me. But we weren't spoiled. Victoria also made us groom the horses and muck the stalls."

A line appeared on the bridge above his nose. And she had the irrational urge to smooth the crease with the tip of her finger. Instead, she stuck her hand in her coat pocket lest she give in to the temptation to touch him.

He flicked the reins, urging the team along. "I don't think material possessions and character have to be an either-or proposition."

She sighed. "Unfortunately there are far too many in my crowd about which that's probably true. Within my own family," she added under her breath.

He pulled the horses up short. "I've been guilty of jumping to wrong conclusions, too. But unless they've walked in your—*ahem*—high heels, people shouldn't judge."

She blinked. "Why, Jonas, did you just make a joke?"

He flicked his eyes at her. "Maybe."

She nudged his shoulder. "I'm impressed."

He gave her a crooked smile. And she put her

hand over her chest, fearing her heart might explode. Mission accomplished. Jonas-Stone smile achieved.

Wow. Just wow.

Maybe it was better he didn't smile often. Even a small smile from him did dangerous things to her nerve endings. He should come with warning labels.

"You know what they say about animals and kids, AnnaBeth."

She tore herself from joyful cowboy dreams. "What do they say?"

"Animals and kids are the best judges of character. To Hunter, you're in a top tier that has nothing to do with money." He returned the shoulder nudge. "You're okay." A lopsided grin this time. "For a flatlander."

"Why, Jonas, darlin'." She batted her eyes at him. "How lovely of you to say so."

He laughed, as she'd meant him to. She didn't think he laughed enough. Perhaps because of whatever happened with Hunter's mom.

At the thought of Kasey Stone, her good mood seeped away. Jonas must be one of those lifers— a one-woman man.

Maybe they'd had one of those soul-mate relationships. The kind of love she'd longed for her whole life but never found.

Which made her sad. Not only for Jonas and

Hunter. But also for other women like herself who were looking for a one-man, cowboy love of their own.

"Sweet potatoes," she muttered.

Jonas looked at her funny. "You okay?"

Immediately, she screwed her face into a semblance of cheerfulness. "I'm great. What else can I do to help you?"

Nobody liked a Gloomy Gus, Victoria always said. Another Victoria-ism—fake it 'til you make it.

He scowled, dimming her optimism. "I asked about the horses because you can either steer the team around the pasture, or break open the bales and throw the hay over the side."

She wasn't sure what had set him off this time. They'd been getting along so well, talking freely, like they were friends and not mere acquaintances a freak snowstorm had inconveniently thrown together.

Perhaps he'd had too much AnnaBeth time. She'd been told she had that effect on people. Maybe they both needed space.

"If it's just the same to you, I think I'll..." Moving toward the bale, she snagged a handful of hay. "Throw it onto the ground, right?"

His handsome mouth resembled the flat line on a hospital heart monitor—the same disapproving way he'd first looked at her when he nearly ran her down. And realized he was going to have to take her home with him.

"Like this?" She went from one side of the wagon to the other, tossing the hay onto the ground.

Drawing closer, the herd munched the fresh, clean feed.

"Stop."

"What?" She froze in midmotion. "What am I doing wrong?"

After tying the reins around the railing, he clambered over to her.

"I'm sorry, Jonas." She felt near tears. Must she always be so useless?

When he took hold of her clenched fist, she gasped. Her hand quivered in his large palm.

"Put on your gloves. I don't want you to hurt yourself." Gently, he pried open her fingers, one by one, until the hay fell to the wagon floor. "Your hands are too pretty to get scratched up like mine, AnnaBeth."

"I like your hands."

Her mouth snapped shut. Her stomach wrenched. Had she actually said that out loud?

But he gave her a soft, slow smile. And her knees nearly buckled.

"That's mighty sweet of you to say, AnnaBeth."

She really, really liked hearing her name on his lips.

His powerful shoulders rose and fell. "I'm nothing special." His gaze fell to her fingers. "Mine are just cowboy hands."

AnnaBeth's heart skipped a beat.

When he brought her hand to his mouth, she believed she might die of happiness right there, surrounded by snuffling horses and scratchy hay bales.

He brushed his lips against her knuckles and held them there for a long second. "Gloves, AnnaBeth," he rasped against her skin.

She felt light-headed all of a sudden. "Okey-dokey…"

Was she a teenager or what? She made a living with her words. But Jonas Stone never failed to reduce her to a fluttery pool of melted goo.

Still, he hadn't let go of her hand.

Get a hold of yourself, girl. Before you say something else totally inane and pointless.

She pulled her hand free.

"Right." He straightened. "Back to work."

She slipped her gloves over her fingers, tingling from the remembered touch of his lips. And while he drove a wide circle around the pasture, she spread hay like nobody's business. Like the best flatlander cowgirl he'd ever see.

Eventually, they off-loaded the hay, and he brought the team back to the barn.

She jumped down and held the bridle for him again. "What about Culpepper and Finian?"

"Like me, these two prefer to stick closer to home." He unharnessed the horses. "I'm going to put them into their stalls." Taking hold of their bridles, he led the horses into the barn.

She followed him inside, and untacked Finian while he untacked Culpepper. After grooming the horses, they forked hay into the stalls.

AnnaBeth was feeling pretty good about her brand-new skills. Until Jonas's next words.

"Why is it you've never asked about Hunter's mother?"

Did she truly want to hear Jonas mourn the whip-thin, blond cowgirl in the photo on Hunter's bookcase?

Her heart dropped to her stomach.

Shutting Finian into his stall, Jonas became unnerved by AnnaBeth's unaccustomed silence. Her emerald eyes had darkened, and her face had become unreadable.

He decided to rephrase—in case she hadn't heard him the first time. "You've never asked about Hunter's mother."

AnnaBeth pursed her lips. "Not any of my business." She spread the blanket across Culpepper's broad back.

He folded his arms. "I'm okay talking about it."

She narrowed her eyes. "Oh, really?"

Disliking her implication, he jutted his jaw. "Really."

At least, when it came to a certain runaway bride.

Shy and reserved by nature, he'd never be accused of being the life of the party. Unlike his good friend Ethan Green. But he did know confidences begat confidences. There was so much about AnnaBeth he didn't know...that he wanted to know.

Info she'd chosen not to reveal about herself. Like earlier when clearly something she was thinking had clouded her face. But when he'd asked her what was wrong, she'd put on the Little-Mary-Sunshine routine she'd perfected to an art form.

And he didn't like it—not when she kept him at arm's length. On the same shallow, need-to-know footing people reserved for mere acquaintances. Going-nowhere relationships.

He sucked in a breath. Is that what he wanted? A relationship? With AnnaBeth?

Jonas scrubbed his hand over his face. No matter the chemistry between them, his heart was in Truelove, at the FieldStone.

And who knew where her heart lay?

Rocking on her heels, she crossed her arms over her coat. "Why tell *me* about your wife, Jonas?"

"Because…" He took a deep breath. "Despite being a chatterbox—"

She gave him a look. "You're going to say something complimentary next, right?"

His mouth curved. He was doing that a lot lately…whenever he was around AnnaBeth.

"Despite being a chatterbox—"

He waited a half second, just to raise her dander. He wasn't disappointed. Her cheeks went pink. Redheads were *so* fun to provoke.

"—you, AnnaBeth Cummings, are a good listener. I feel comfortable talking with you."

"I'm safe." She nodded. "I get that a lot."

He frowned. That wasn't what he meant.

But this was why he didn't talk more, especially to women. They often misinterpreted even the simplest of conversations.

He scowled. "No, AnnaBeth—"

"Yes, Jonas…" She lifted her chin. "It's okay. I feel safe with you, too." She smiled.

AnnaBeth felt *safe* with him? That was good, right? Then why did he somehow feel insulted?

Somewhere this entire conversation had gone off the rails. And he wasn't sure how to get it back on track. It was like she was trying to distract and confuse him. Deliberately veer him off-topic. But why?

He lifted his hat, then resettled it on his head. "I mean, I'd like to think we're friends, AnnaBeth."

She arched an eyebrow. "Friends?"

"I could use a friend." He shuffled his boots. "I'm guessing you could probably use a friend, too."

Jonas was nothing if not rational. He couldn't afford to get too invested in her. Nor her in him. Friendship made much more sense. It was the only option either of them could or should consider.

Having sorted it out in his mind, he already felt better about the situation.

Friends. That's what they'd be. Problem solved.

As for the unnamed feelings he'd been experiencing since meeting her, he reassured himself only a complete idiot wouldn't empathize with someone who found themselves in a similar circumstance.

Right. Good. Glad he'd got that squared away. Except, she hadn't said anything. *Not good.*

Instead, she stared at him like he'd suddenly grown horns.

Earlier, when his son had asked Jonas to be AnnaBeth's friend, Jonas had looked as if he'd prefer to do anything—short of torture and death—than be her friend.

Why the change of heart?

Other than the fact he now wanted to talk about his late, great, dead wife?

"Sweet potatoes," she muttered.

Jonas looked at her.

And when he gazed at her with those melted-chocolate eyes of his, she couldn't help but go all instant pudding on him.

There's not going to be a way to dodge this bullet, is there, God?

Jonas, spilling his guts about his lost love. Remorse pricked her conscience.

Stoic, aloof Jonas admitted he needed a friend. Which obviously meant he trusted her if he was ready to tell her his life story. She should be flattered.

Why wasn't she flattered that Jonas wanted to be her friend?

"AnnaBeth?"

She refocused. And reconciled herself to yet another Tell-Me-About-Your-Romance-with-Another-Woman conversation.

AnnaBeth moistened her bottom lip. "Hunter showed me the photo of his mother. He said her name was Kasey."

When a shadow passed over his face, AnnaBeth felt it like a punch to the gut.

The mere mention of his wife's name… Jonas still loved Kasey so much.

He looked away. Jonas couldn't even look her in the eye and tell the story of his one true love.

"Kasey and I met on the rodeo circuit."

Then he stalled. Apparently, she'd also need to prompt him through the story.

"You rode broncos."

Jonas nodded. "My wife—"

He blew out a breath. "Kasey had spent her life on the circuit. Her parents were well-known in rodeo circles. She did barrel racing."

"Sounds dangerous."

He rubbed his neck. "But therein lies the thrill."

"I'm sure it's an adrenaline rush."

Whereas her idea of an adrenaline rush was wearing white shoes before Easter.

"After a while, I lost the taste for rodeoing. Too much to live for outside the arena."

She wasn't sure how she should respond to that, so she kept quiet.

His gaze flickered over the snow-dappled ridge. "I'm ashamed to tell you the rest. It does me no credit, but I fell away from God during those years on the circuit." His Adam's apple bobbed. "Kasey and I… She got pregnant."

AnnaBeth hadn't seen that coming. But Jonas's eyes found hers, waiting for her reaction.

Careful of her expression, she kept her composure. She put on the game face she'd learned in cotillion. "It happens."

He squared his jaw. "I was determined to do right by her and the baby, but she didn't want to be tied down."

AnnaBeth laced her hands together. "Children have a tendency to do that."

"It was only with a great deal of reluctance she finally agreed to marry me. I think she knew, even if I was too pigheaded to see it, that we weren't compatible. That we wouldn't be happy together."

The remorse in his voice, the pain on his face, broke her heart. "You're not that same man, Jonas. I can tell."

"I was so selfish, AnnaBeth. After Hunter was born, I stood it as long as I could, but we fought a lot." He sucked in a breath. "There was this one bronc… Not merely a cliché. My life flashed in front of my eyes, and I knew I had to be done with the rodeo for my son's sake."

AnnaBeth wasn't sure where he was going.

"I wanted to come home to help Mom run the ranch, but Kasey told me if I seriously thought she'd ever live on this backwater mountain hollow, I could think again."

AnnaBeth stopped breathing.

"She told me she'd rather die than leave her career. And unfortunately, that's exactly what she did. She died. The divorce hadn't yet been finalized before she got herself killed in a stupid rodeo stunt."

Her tongue felt thick in her throat. "How old was Hunter when…? When she…?"

"It's okay to say it, AnnaBeth. She left me.

've come to grips with her deserting me." He ran his hand over his head. "It's been harder getting over her abandoning her son." His mouth thinned. "Hunter wasn't yet eight months old."

AnnaBeth put her hand on his arm, desperate to offer him at least a small shred of comfort. To erase the look of inadequacy on his face. A feeling she knew all too well.

"I'm sorry, Jonas."

"Hunter and I have been on our own ever since. I don't know how I would've made it the first two years without Mom. But lately, I worry she's sacrificing too much for us. Especially since she and Dwight Fleming have started spending so much time together."

"You know about that?"

"I may be clueless most of the time, but I'm not totally oblivious." He grimaced. "I'm afraid she's putting aside her own happiness to stay at the ranch and take care of us."

"She loves you both. Devotedly."

He sighed. "If only every mother was as good a mother as my mom. I blame myself for what happened with Kasey."

But AnnaBeth had a hard time understanding how a mother could leave her baby.

She took hold of his hand. "I do that, too. But don't blame yourself."

"When I met her, I knew the rodeo was Kas-

ey's whole world. But the FieldStone Ranch wa
everything I really wanted. Different worlds. Dif
ferent dreams. Different goals."

Over the years, she'd pieced together a simila
story in her parents' marriage. But it had bee
her father's all-consuming ambition to climb th
banking ladder and his relentless drive towar
perfection that split her parents apart. Her mon
hadn't fit into his image of the corporate wife.

As for being the perfect corporate daughter
AnnaBeth had the suspicion that, despite Victo
ria's best efforts over the years, neither had she.

She had no concrete memories of them togethe
as a family. She'd been so young when her mothe
died. Then she'd gone to live with her father an
Victoria.

"Thank you for sharing that with me, Jonas.
appreciate how painful it is to share those kind o
wounds with someone."

"You're a pretty terrific listener, AnnaBeth
And you're not just someone. You're a friend
know I can trust." His eyes bored into hers. "I'n
so grateful you came into our lives."

Jonas felt grateful to have her there?

"The change you've wrought in Hunter..." H
squared his jaw. "You've shown me I need t
make some changes in my life. For his sake."

For Hunter's sake. *Right.*

"If you ever want to talk about what happened with your fiancé, I'm willing to listen."

About how humiliated she'd felt in losing Scott to her baby sister? *So not happening.* Although, what would be the harm in leaving out that one measly detail? What would it hurt?

She still had her pride. She'd do almost anything to avoid Jonas feeling sorry for her. She wasn't ready for full disclosure. Not just yet.

They were friends. Just friends. It wasn't like it mattered that she tell him everything.

Yet he was obviously waiting for her to say something. She had to say something. Anything…

"I've been burned by love." Painting a smile on her face, she said the polite, distancing thing Southern girls learned in the cradle. "But I'll be fine."

He scowled. "Stop doing that."

"Stop doing what?"

"You know what. The My-Smile-is-My-Armor thing you do." He glared. "It may play in Charlotte, but you don't fool me. You don't have to fake being happy with me, AnnaBeth, when you're not."

She glared at him. "Happy? What's not to be happy about? I'm happy." She clenched her teeth. "So, so happy."

"You were jilted at the altar by the man you loved, AnnaBeth."

"I didn't love Scott."

"You didn't love him?" Jonas's eyes widened "And you were going to marry him, anyway?"

How to explain something she didn't quite understand herself…

"It meant so much to Daddy. He and Scott's father are best friends. Scott and I have known each other since we were children. And Victoria got so excited about the wedding, she went all stepmother-zilla."

"AnnaBeth…"

She shrugged. "I wasn't in love with anyone else. At the time, neither was he. It seemed…"

"It seemed what, AnnaBeth?" Jonas grunted.

"Easier."

He gaped at her. "Easier than what? Tying yourself to someone you don't love for the rest of your life? You deserve better than that."

That's what Jonas didn't get. And she wasn't about to tell him otherwise. Even after all these years, her father couldn't speak her mother's name without losing his temper.

And though outwardly picture-perfect, his marriage the second time around was nothing to write home about, either.

"What kind of person does that? Marries someone they don't love?"

She lifted her chin. "Where I come from, lots of people do."

Based on the heated exchanges she'd overheard through the years, she was fairly certain her father married Victoria because of her family connections. And for the first time, she felt a vague feeling of pity for her stepmother.

Jonas's mouth flattened. "How could you ever think you'd be satisfied with that?" He moved closer.

So close she felt his breath flutter a strand of hair dangling at her earlobe. Her heart stutter-stepped.

How? Because she'd never dreamed anyone like Jonas could ever make her feel so...valued? Special?

"You deserve more, so much more. If only you would see yourself the way I see you..."

How did Jonas see her?

As a friend? Good with children? Blogger extraordinaire? Or was he trying to tell her something else?

But, lacking the courage to ask, she stepped away. From the point of no return. Before she made a fool out of herself and discovered he wasn't feeling the words she longed for him to say.

"Looks like we both have trust issues." She folded her arms around herself. "We should probably go back to the lodge."

The sun had begun its slow descent toward the

ridge. As she'd discovered last night, night came quickly in the Blue Ridge Mountains.

"Your mom and Hunter are probably wondering where we are."

He picked up the reins. "Not every man is like Scott. And not every man has a problem with commitment."

"No?" She cocked her head. "Maybe you should take your own advice."

Scowling, he flicked the reins and put the team in motion, setting her teeth to rattling almost as much as he'd already rattled her heart.

Chapter Eight

The next morning, Jonas drove to the far pasture, parking as close as he could get to the downed fence.

During the storm, a huge, snow-laden branch had broken off from an overhanging oak. And when it fell, the branch took down an entire section of barbed wire. Breath fogging the air, he dragged the tree off the wire.

The sun was shining, but the temperature wasn't warming. At this rate, the snow would remain on the ground for a long time.

Was he actually starting to hope the roads would keep their runaway bride stranded on the FieldStone indefinitely?

He growled low in his throat. What a chump. She'd pushed him away yesterday when he'd been trying to be a friend.

Because he'd decided that's all they could

be. Friendship was all he wanted from Anna-Beth. *Right?*

He wasn't sure how she could make him fee so at ease and yet so off-kilter at the same time.

Protective earphones slung around his neck, he retrieved the chain saw from the truck bed. Ear phones and face shield in place, he spent a hal hour cutting up the stout branch. And despite the chill, it didn't take long for him to shed his coat.

The roar of the chain saw drowned all othe sounds, giving him ample time to reflect on the events of the last few days. And the one person who occupied his every waking thought.

By sharing the pain of his past failures, he'd hoped to encourage AnnaBeth to trust him and do the same—open up about what had to have been the most painful day of her life. When he no-good fiancé left her at the altar.

Good thing her sorry ex-fiancé didn't live any where near Truelove. She could say what she liked about not being in love with Scott. Jonas wasn't so sure she didn't still have feelings for him.

Jonas wasn't a violent man, but when he con templated how humiliated AnnaBeth must've felt to run away from her family in the middle of a snowstorm…

His left hand tightened on the front handle. I not for God's watchful care, she could have eas ily lost her life.

The save-a-life connection must be real. Otherwise, he had no explanation for the intense feeling of protectiveness he felt for her.

Across the snowy terrain, a flash of gold drew his attention. Dwight Fleming's SUV rounded the curve in the driveway. The road to town must be clear again. And it appeared his mother had a gentleman caller.

Dwight was a great guy. Barring snowstorms, there weren't many days his mother and Dwight didn't keep company.

He was glad his mother had someone special in her life again. Which turned his mind to the lovely flatlander. And less happily, also to the last someone he'd had in his life.

From what he'd observed of AnnaBeth over the last couple of days, he had a strong feeling no one could have pried her child from her. Nor would she have willingly walked away.

When he watched her with Hunter, his heart felt like it was lodged in his throat. Someday, she would make someone a wonderful mother, a wonderful wife.

The lump in his throat grew. Wife to him? No... Not him. He was done with relationships. Yet there was such a beguiling sweetness to AnnaBeth.

Unbidden, an image rose to his mind of a sunny autumn day in a mountain meadow. AnnaBeth's laughing, happy face. Her belly big with child. His child?

His heart hammered. As he lifted the saw off the wood, he activated the brake. What was he thinking?

They came from such different worlds. And AnnaBeth deserved someone wonderful. With so much more to offer than he ever could.

His chin dropped. Throttling up once more, he cut the branch into shorter lengths he'd haul to the firebox at the house. He needed to think about something other than the flatlander...

She was nothing like Kasey. Somehow he sensed that when AnnaBeth loved someone, she loved deeply and forever.

His lip curled. That Scott dude didn't know what a treasure he'd let slip through his fingers.

When the chain saw stopped cutting smoothly, he activated the brake. Lifting the face shield, he took a closer look.

Great. If it wasn't one thing, it was twelve. The tension was off. The chain must be too loose.

Jonas had just set the saw on the tailgate to tighten the chain when a shout of laughter drew his attention to the hill behind the barn. He smiled.

His son had found yet another way to enjoy winter fun. Cheeks rosy from the cold, AnnaBeth cheered wildly as Hunter sledded downhill on the saucerlike lid of a trash can.

It did something good to his heart to see his son so happy. AnnaBeth was like that, though. She had the ability to bring sunshine and warmth to even a gray day.

Jonas clambered onto the truck bed, but despite his best intentions, his gaze strayed toward the fun happening across the pasture.

Hunter zoomed down the hill. Bottoming out, he trudged back up the incline over and over again. Several times, the plastic lid dumped his little cowboy topsy-turvy onto the snow, but each time, he jumped up laughing.

"I'm going to go faster, AnnaBef," his son yelled. "Watch me! Watch me fwy!"

Jonas smiled at the joy in his son's voice. He surveyed the long length of the fence yet to be repaired. His heart wasn't into it today. Wasn't like he was getting much done, anyway—

"Hunter!" AnnaBeth yelled. "Watch out!" She screamed. "Hunter!"

Scrambling off the tailgate, he ran toward the sounds of AnnaBeth's screams. A second. He'd taken his eyes off them for only a second.

But sometimes, a second was the only difference between well-being and tragedy.

They'd been having fun until Hunter hit a slick patch of snow under the shade of a lone pine.

Ice had sent the saucer veering completely off

course, and the makeshift sled had careened into a big boulder. Thrown out, Hunter skittered on his backside a great distance before coming to rest in a bowl-shaped dip in the land.

AnnaBeth ran down the hill.

Testing his limbs, Hunter slowly got to his feet. He grinned at her. "I'm okay." He stuck his thumb to his chest. "Cowboy-tough."

She put her hand over her pounding heart. "You scared me, sweetie pie. That was a bad tumble. Are you sure...?"

Tiny, spiderweb-like fractures appeared on the snow-covered ground around him, radiating with a horrifying suddenness.

His eyes rounded at the same instant she realized he'd landed in the middle of a frozen pond. There was a loud, echoing crack. Hunter fell through the ice into the circle of water. And then he went under.

Terror-stricken, she screamed, "Hunter!"

His head bobbed to the surface. Arms flailing, he sputtered, "AnnaBef!"

"Stay here." Hat flying off his head, Jonas rushed past her. "I've got him."

"Wait, Jonas. If Hunter was too heavy—"

But reaching the edge of the pond, Jonas lay flat on his stomach to better distribute his weight. "Hang on, Hunter. Daddy's coming." He slowly inched forward. "Don't panic. Remember your swim lessons last summer."

She held her breath.

Dog-paddling, Hunter lifted his head to keep his face out of the water. "I—I so c-c-cold-d D-D-Dad-d-dy."

Flat on his belly, Jonas stretched his arms toward his son. "I've got you. Daddy's—"

The ice underneath him shattered.

Jonas plunged into the freezing cold pond. Both of them went under. And she thought her heart might stop from fear.

Like a cork, though, Jonas popped to the top, holding Hunter tight against him. But after being dunked for the second time, Hunter had gone into full-blown panic.

If Hunter didn't drown Jonas first, it wouldn't be long before his limbs would begin to feel weighted and grow numb.

She had to do something…fast. He wouldn't be able to keep them afloat for long.

Maybe there was something in the truck she could use to help them.

She turned on her heel and raced toward the hill. Rounding the top, she dashed toward the truck parked near the fence line.

Flinging herself over the tailgate, she spotted a rope coiled near the toolbox. Grabbing it, she jumped over the side and sped to the pond. "Please, God. Don't let me be too late."

Slipping and sliding, she crashed through the snow. Reaching the bottom of the hill, she tied one end of the rope around the trunk of the pine tree.

"I'm coming!" she yelled. "Hang on, Jonas. Hang on, Hunt." Keeping hold of the other end of the rope, she took off for the pond.

Legs wrapped around Jonas's torso, Hunter clung to his father. But she could see the strain in Jonas's face. The effort it was costing him to keep both their heads above the surface of the water.

Going as far as she dared, she took a deep breath. Suppose she missed? But there was no time to lose. She couldn't miss. She had to get the rope to them, as fast as she could, on the first try.

Remembering what Hunter had taught her, she tossed the rope onto the ice. It landed with a plop in the widening circle of water in front of Jonas. Holding Hunter with one arm against himself, Jonas snagged the rope.

She breathed a sigh of relief. *Thank You, God. Thank You.*

A split second later, Jonas noosed the rope around Hunter's midsection.

"What are you—?"

"You're not strong enough to pull us both out at the same time," he called.

"But what about you?"

"Don't worry about me. Just get my son to safety."

But she cared about Jonas… Far more than she should… She couldn't leave him in the water. There wasn't time for a second throw.

And from the grim, resigned look on his face, he knew the truth, too.

"Now, AnnaBeth. Pull!" he shouted. "Save my son!"

God, help me. Help me save both of them. Please…

There was a shout from behind her. An older man came charging over the hill. And behind him, Deirdre.

Skidding to a stop, the fiftysomething man grabbed onto another section of the taut line in AnnaBeth's hands. "It'll take all of us," he grunted.

Out of breath, Deirdre took a spot between them. "We saw what happened from the terrace."

"Jonas!" the man shouted. "Get ready! We've only got one shot at this. We're hauling both of you out on the count of three."

AnnaBeth tightened her grip.

"Ready," the man warned. "One… Two… Three. Pull!"

Hang on, Jonas. His muscles had to be so fatigued. *Don't let his arms give out, God.*

Digging in her heels, she fought with all her strength to maintain her grip. A desperate tug-of-war. A matter of life and death. She bit her lip so hard, she tasted the metallic taste of her own blood.

Gaining traction, the man repositioned his hands. "Heave!" he grunted.

Hanging on to the rope, Jonas and Hunter cleared the edge of the ice.

"Again!" Deirdre shouted.

Her arms felt as if they were on fire, but AnnaBeth didn't dare slacken her hold. Straining. Holding on for dear life—the lives of Hunter and Jonas. Dearer to her than her own.

One mighty yank and they were out of the water.

"Don't move!" the man yelled. "The ice is unstable. Let us pull you to safety."

Hand over hand, they tugged, bringing Jonas and Hunter closer. Until at last, they dragged them off the frozen pond and onto stable ground. Only then did she let go of the rope.

Chest heaving, Jonas was lying in the snow, his arms in a death grip around his son.

"I'm sowee, Dad." Hunter sobbed. "I'm sowee."

He touched Hunter's face. "Not your fault, son. An—an accident." Spent beyond measure, his hand fell.

Soaking wet, they shivered uncontrollably with the first signs of hypothermia.

The older man shrugged out of his coat and handed it to Deirdre. "Not been cold long enough yet this season to freeze the pond solid through."

Deirdre ran forward with the coat, but Jonas waved her off. "H-Hunt…"

She wrapped the big, burly jacket around Hunter's small frame. His sobs had turned into hiccups.

"Jonas…" AnnaBeth fell to her knees beside him in the snow. "Are you all right? Jonas?" His lips were blue. His face, so pale.

And she couldn't seem to keep from touching him. Reassuring herself he was alive. Her mitten brushed over his wet hair. Touched his hand. His cheek.

Something in his dark eyes gentled. "I'm fine. Thanks to your quick action."

"Not me." She fluttered her hand. "If they hadn't arrived when they did…" She'd been so close to losing them both. Too close.

She flushed. Her losing them? They weren't ever hers to lose in the first place.

Now that the danger was over, Deirdre sagged against the man. "The Lord is good." She twined her fingers with the man's. "God knew we'd need Dwight's help today."

Dwight squeezed her hand.

With an athletic build, he had the kind of classic

handsomeness that with certain men never fades. Not unlike her own father.

Her eyes tremulous, Deirdre smiled at Dwight.

One eyebrow raised, AnnaBeth caught Jonas's eye.

He winked. "Don't make me get my shotgun, Mom."

Dwight laughed.

Lips twitching, Jonas's mother planted her hands on her hips. "Don't think 'cause you almost drowned, you're too big for me to put over my knee, mister."

Jonas grinned. And AnnaBeth's heart did the familiar flutter thing it did whenever Jonas smiled.

She got to her feet. Too quickly. For a moment, the world spun. Either that, or that killer smile of his.

It might have been her imagination and she wasn't sure why, but it seemed over the last few days, Jonas smiled more often.

Cocking his head, he held out his hand to her. "If you've got any strength left, I could use a little help getting off the ground."

She grasped his hand, widened her stance and tugged him upright.

"Thanks." Eyebrows bunching, he motioned to her bottom lip. "What happened there?"

"AnnaBef!"

When Hunter threw himself at her, she staggered. His arms locked around her legs—she would've gone down, except for Jonas's steadying hand.

She bent over Hunter. "Sweetie pie."

And when Jonas joined his mother and Dwight, she felt bereft, strangely abandoned. Ridiculous since she'd been the one to move away from him. Like yesterday, when they were feeding the horses.

But now, as then, she figured it was best not to get too used to something she could never have. Only make parting that much harder.

Warming Hunter's face between her gloves, she cuddled him closer, trying to share her body heat with him.

"Are you sure, you're not hurting anywhere? Does your tummy hurt?" She glanced over to Hunter's grandmother. "He might've swallowed pond water."

She was disturbed to find Jonas's gaze boring into her. The gentle look had been replaced by something she didn't altogether understand.

He folded his arms over his wet shirt. "It wouldn't be a bad idea to get him checked out." His voice gruff, he was once more retreating to the place inside himself where he kept his feelings locked.

Dwight rubbed his chin. "The road to town is plowed, but I can't say the same about heading over the ridge to the medical center. Amber could look him over, though. What do you think?"

Amber? AnnaBeth's stomach knotted. Did Jonas have a girlfriend?

"Good idea. My truck's over the rise." He motioned. "And my coat."

Deirdre patted his shoulder. "Before you head out, let's get you both some dry clothes."

The men tromped off to retrieve the truck. And, hand in hand with Hunter, the women plodded toward the house.

"In case you're wondering, honeybun, Amber is Dwight's daughter and a pediatric nurse."

AnnaBeth bit her lip. "I wasn't. Wondering."

Deirdre arched an eyebrow. As if she didn't believe her. "Amber and her husband, Ethan Green—"

Amber had a husband?

"—live near town with their twin daughters. Ethan's grandmother, ErmaJean, is best friends with my aunt IdaLee." Deirdre gave AnnaBeth a significant look.

Any significance, however, was lost on AnnaBeth.

But she nodded as if she understood. "I'm guessing Dwight is the man I've heard you talking to on the phone every night."

Spots of color bloomed in Deirdre's cheeks.

And AnnaBeth envisioned how Jonas's mother must've looked as a girl.

Deirdre tried not to smile. And failed. "Both of us are widowed. His wife, Kitty, was actually my closest friend. Last fall, we found ourselves running into each other all over town." She dropped her gaze to the path. "Silly, isn't it? At our age."

"I think it's wonderful."

Deirdre darted her eyes at AnnaBeth.

"I hope you'll invite me to the wedding."

Letting go of Hunter's hand, despite the frigid temperature, Deirdre fanned her face. "We keep each other company, but it's not like that."

For a second, AnnaBeth imagined an autumn wedding set on the FieldStone Ranch. And the tasteful, elegant touches Victoria would include. Showcasing the ranch and the splendor of the Blue Ridge Mountains.

There was no denying it, her stepmother was nothing if not classy.

Slipping into the kitchen, she held the door for Deirdre and Hunter. "Your relationship with Dwight sure looks like something to me."

Deirdre motioned Hunter to the back staircase. "Run upstairs and put on dry clothes, honey. Gramma will be there in a minute."

He climbed the stairs slower than his usual

breakneck speed. The cold had sapped him of his energy, leaving him drooping.

They watched him until he disappeared from view.

"Why not, Deirdre?"

She shook her head, but a fond smile played about her lips. "You're like a dog with a bone when you get your teeth into something, aren't you, honeybun?"

AnnaBeth flicked her hand. "Quit stalling and answer the question."

"Why not? Without a mother, Hunter needs me. And I can't in good conscience leave Jonas to manage the ranch by himself. He needs a wife." Deirdre flicked a look in AnnaBeth's direction. "And I'm thinking you might be the very one to apply for the job. What do you say?"

Mouth gaping open, AnnaBeth took a step backward. "I—I…"

Wow. That escalated fast. These mountain folk were nothing if not direct.

"Ummmm…" AnnaBeth made for the stairs. "Why don't I go check on Hunter?"

"Run all you like, honeybun, but you can't hide." Her soft laughter followed AnnaBeth's hasty retreat. "I have it on good authority Aunt IdaLee and the matchmakers have a new project. A *Christmas* project."

Chapter Nine

Sitting beside AnnaBeth in the truck, Jonas waited for Hunter to join them. When he stopped to consider what nearly happened to his son at the pond...

He wrapped his hands around the wheel to stop their shaking. God was so good. And if not for her quick thinking, today could've so easily ended in a tragedy from which he would never have recovered.

Not just for a little boy's Christmas wish, but perhaps the real reason God had brought Anna-Beth to the FieldStone was to rescue them today.

Cutting his eyes at her, he was disconcerted to find her gaze locked onto his.

"You're been through so much. Do you need me to drive, Jonas?"

How did she know what he was feeling? She read him so well. Not many people did.

"I—I…" His face burning, he hoped she really didn't see everything he was feeling. Not when it came to her. "You saved our lives."

She gave him a quick, shy glance before dropping her gaze. "We saved each other." Holding his hat in her lap, she ran her finger over the suede fabric. "I guess we're even now, huh?"

"I'm totally in your debt." He raked his hand over his head. "I could never repay you for the life of my son," he grunted.

A pucker formed between her brows. He had the irrational urge to trace his finger over the delicate curve of her eyebrow.

"Jonas—"

Dwight wrenched open the truck door. "Hunter's all set to go."

Having donned his cowboy hat and boots, Hunter scrambled into the truck. Draping her arm around his son, she snuggled him close.

"Deirdre's on the phone with your aunt." Leaning inside the cab, Dwight made sure the buckle on the booster seat was securely fastened around Hunter. "I called Amber to let her know you were coming."

"Thanks, Dwight." His eyes blurred. It wasn't like him to get emotional. "For everything."

Smiling, Dwight stepped back. "I'm going to visit with your mom. You know to drive careful on these mountain roads. Any melted snow will refreeze once darkness falls."

Jonas reached for the ignition. "I'll take care. I hope we won't be gone too long."

Heading down the drive, he threaded the truck through the stone gateposts and onto the road.

AnnaBeth sighed. "Hunter's gone to sleep."

Head lolling against AnnaBeth's shoulder, his hat had fallen forward over his forehead. "Is he okay?"

"I think so." She didn't move her arm. If anything, her arm tightened around his son. "He's probably just exhausted from the ordeal."

Jonas blew out a breath. "He's not the only one. I've probably aged a decade since this morning." Halfway down the mountain, he pointed toward the side of the road. "Zach's towed your car."

She turned her head at the empty space where she'd been forced to abandon her vehicle.

"After we get Hunter checked out and buy some more cold medication for Mom, we should ride over to his shop on Main." He glanced at her. "Get the verdict on your car."

She nodded. "And with me gone, your life can finally return to normal."

Normal hadn't been so good for him. Since AnnaBeth's arrival, his life had taken a definite upswing. But based on what happened and what didn't between them yesterday in the pasture, she didn't feel the same way.

"I'm sure you can't wait to be rid of us." He looked at her. "And eager to see your family."

She stared through the windshield at the winding road. "Not so much, actually."

Not so much to be rid of them? Or, not so much to see her family?

Her blog tagline read, "May your heart always know the way home."

But was AnnaBeth still searching for her heart's home? And an even more disquieting notion...

Despite everything he thought he believed about himself, for the first time in his life, Jonas wondered if he'd truly found his.

Reaching the valley, the road leveled off. The Department of Transportation had been busy. Piles of plowed snow dotted the sides of the road.

The truck rattled over the bridge.

"Dwight runs a river-rafting company during the spring, summer and fall. Same seasons as the FieldStone. His son-in-law, Ethan, is a good friend of mine."

She straightened to get a better look at the boulder-studded river that flowed beneath the bridge. The scent of roses wafted across his nostrils.

His heart thudded. "I don't guess that first day you made it as far as town."

She rolled her eyes. "If there's a wrong path to

take, you can be assured I'll find it. Wrong-Way Cummings, that's me."

From where he was sitting—alive and with his son—she had taken exactly the right road.

"You'll meet their twin girls, Lucy and Stella, from Amber's first marriage."

"So Ethan is their stepfather?"

There was that weird note in her voice again. Every time step-anything was mentioned. Not for the first time, he wondered about her relationship with her stepmother. And with her father.

"Amber jokes Ethan only married her because he loves the girls so much. And the feeling is mutual. Lucy and Stella are wild about him." Jonas grinned. "Actually, the twins can be a little wild. Period."

She smiled. "Twins. How fun."

On the outskirts of town, she swiveled to read the Welcome-to-Truelove sign. "Where True Love Awaits." She blinked. "So that's really a thing here?"

"You have no idea." And then he remembered who else she was likely to encounter at Ethan's. "About that…"

"About what?" Her eyes widened. "True love?"

"Yes, I mean, no. Well, not exactly. Sort of," he stammered.

She laughed. He flushed.

"You're going to meet Ethan's grandma, too.

But the thing is, ErmaJean and her friends, including my great-aunt IdaLee, get these outrageous ideas."

Each word a potential land mine, he kept his explanation of the Truelove Matchmakers and their shenanigans as brief as possible.

"I see. You don't want Ethan's grandmother to get the wrong idea about you and me." AnnaBeth's gaze became remote. "I'll try not to embarrass you in front of your friends."

"That's not what—"

Nearly overshooting Ethan's bungalow, he had to abruptly swerve into the driveway. AnnaBeth put her hand on the dashboard to brace.

"Sorry," he grunted.

Jonas parked and shut off the engine.

Hunter awoke with a start. "Are we here yet, Dad?" His little guy rubbed his eyes.

Giving Jonas a nice view of her shoulder, she fussed over his son. Smoothing her hand over his hair. Touching his cheek.

His mind flew to the look in her eyes when she touched his face at the pond. And he wished... It didn't matter what he wished.

Because she seemed determined to think the worst of him, or because he was jealous of her attention to his son?

His stomach cramped. He'd only met the

woman a few days ago. But sad, mad or glad, she'd managed to make him feel more alive than he'd felt in years.

Jonas got out of the truck and came around the hood, but she'd already managed to free his son from the booster seat.

She shoved Jonas's hat into his chest. "Here." And took Hunter's small hand in hers.

Clamping the hat on his head, he took his son's other hand. "Just so you know…"

She paused, midstep.

"The girls are sweet, but sometimes they overwhelm Hunter."

She sniffed. "Like father like son?"

His mouth tightened. "Yeah. That."

She crinkled her nose. "Good to know."

He bristled. Yet when she flipped her hair over her shoulder, he imagined the sensation of running his fingers through the red silk of her hair. And promptly stumbled over his own feet.

Ethan came out onto the porch. "Dwight said to be on the lookout for you." He waved them over.

But Jonas scowled, annoyed for letting the debutante get under his skin. Again.

Inside the house, Hunter flat-out refused to let Amber Green put her stethoscope to his chest unless AnnaBeth stayed with him.

She exchanged a look with Jonas. "Of course, I'll stay with you, punkin."

Hunter cocked his head. "I'm not a pumpkin, AnnaBef."

She winked. "Sure you are, sweetie pie. Pumpkin pie's my favorite." She flipped her unruly hair over her shoulder again.

Jonas rubbed his hand on the side of his jeans. He'd been doing that a lot since they came inside the bungalow.

Ethan and Amber Green appeared to be a few years younger than Jonas. About her own age. Lucy and Stella resembled their mother. And as Jonas had warned, they swept upon Hunter like a duo of mother hens.

Amber rolled her eyes. "One day you're going to have to beat the girls off this little cowboy with a stick, Jonas."

Ethan snorted. "Any boy hurts one of my girls better think again."

Amber's mouth curved. "Says Mr. Love-'em-and-Leave-'em."

"No more leaving them. Just Mr. Love-'em, honey." He kissed his wife's cheek. "Jonas and I will keep the girls in the kitchen until you're finished."

Seeing the two of them beside their Christmas tree left AnnaBeth with a slightly wistful feeling.

Would her turn ever come? Would God ever send her a love like that?

She kept quiet as Amber listened to Hunter's chest.

Caught in a ponytail, Amber's wheat-blond hair swung from side to side. Straightening, she removed the stethoscope and rehung it around her neck. "His lungs sound clear."

AnnaBeth exhaled. "That's a relief."

Dwight's daughter removed Hunter's hat and, using her fingers, gently probed his skull. "Did he hit his head or lose consciousness?"

"I don't think he lost consciousness." AnnaBeth squeezed his fingers. "Hunter, did you hit your head on the rock or the ice when you fell?"

"Nope. AnnaBef saved me and my dad." Hunter wrinkled his brow. "If I'm good, Miss Amber, do I get a lollipop when you're done?"

"We'll see what we can do." Amber peered into his ear. "I hear it was Hunter and Jonas to the rescue when your car broke down the night of the snowstorm, AnnaBeth."

"How did you—?"

"Small-town grapevine." Amber checked his other ear. "Miss Deirdre told Jonas's great-aunt IdaLee. Miss IdaLee called Miss ErmaJean." Her lips twitched. "From there I'm imagining it went to infinity and beyond."

AnnaBeth felt the telltale heat rising out from

the collar of her cable-knit sweater. If Amber knew about her rescue, chances were the whole town also knew about the runaway-bride thing too.

Hunter opened his mouth, and Amber inserted a tongue depressor. Her blue eyes flitted to Anna-Beth. "Truelove's nothing like where you're from, I'm guessing."

AnnaBeth was starting to feel this wasn't so much Hunter's examination as a personal inquisition. But she didn't mind. Not really.

It was wonderful Jonas had friends who cared about them so much. She wished she had friends like Amber and Ethan. Maybe she wouldn't have agreed to marry a man she didn't love. And the wedding fiasco could have been avoided.

But that would've also meant never meeting Hunter and Jonas. And she'd trade humiliation any day not to have missed the opportunity to know them.

"I haven't seen much of Truelove so far, but if the town is as special as the ranch and the family who owns it—" she lifted her chin "—I can't think of a better place to live."

"Daddy wants to know if you're finished." Lucy popped her head around the door frame. "Are you finished yet, Mommy?"

Amber smiled. "We're finished."

Ethan and Jonas strolled into the living room.

Accompanied by the twins, Ethan's grandmother came out of the kitchen with a plastic container in her arms.

"IdaLee says your mom is under the weather." She handed Jonas the container. "Chicken-and-rice soup will cure what ails her." Her blue eyes twinkled. "That and Dwight Fleming, I daresay."

Ethan introduced AnnaBeth to his grandmother.

"AnnaBeth…" ErmaJean tapped her finger on her chin. "A double name. Isn't that interesting?" A speculative look crossed her face.

Jonas shuffled his boots on the carpet. "How's Hunter, Amber?"

"Looks like he's suffered no ill effects from falling through the ice." Amber ruffled Hunter's hair. "Although, it would be wise to keep an eye out for any unusual symptoms or discomfort over the next twenty-four hours."

"Will do," AnnaBeth helped Hunter pull on his coat. "I'll set my alarm tonight and check on him every few hours."

ErmaJean tilted her head. "You'd do that? For Jonas's son?"

"Of course." She picked up Hunter off the couch. His little boots dangled. "He and I are best buds, right?"

"He's too heavy for you, AnnaBeth." Jonas

moved toward the sofa. "Let me take him. He's a big boy."

"Hunter's had a scary day. And he's not that big." She nuzzled Hunter's hair with her cheek. "Never too big to need cuddling."

ErmaJean smiled. "I can't tell you how delighted I am to make your acquaintance, Anna-Beth Cummings."

And she got the feeling she'd passed a final exam. An exam she hadn't realized she was taking.

"Wasn't sure how it was going to work out when you told Santa what you wanted this year." ErmaJean patted Hunter's leg. "But I think it's going to be a wonderful Christmas."

Something akin to panic filled Jonas's eyes. "Uh… Don't want to outstay our welcome. We really should be—"

"Looks like you got your mommy wish three weeks early, Hunter." ErmaJean pursed her lips.

"Mommy wish?" AnnaBeth swung around to Jonas.

The color in his cheeks rivaling a poinsettia, he quickly hustled them out the door.

Driving away from the Greens' home, Jonas waited with trepidation for a storm of questions to erupt from AnnaBeth.

Instead, she gave his son a bright smile. "Would you like to play a game on my phone?"

Hunter fist-pumped the air. "Yay!"

After digging through her purse, she handed his son her cell phone. She showed him what to do. And other than the pings, bells and whistles emanating from the app, silence reigned in the truck.

But then...

"You said we were going to check on my car, right?"

Wary as a long-tailed cat on a porch full of rocking chairs, he nodded.

"Is your cousin's shop far?"

He headed toward Main Street. "Nothing in Truelove is far from anything."

"While we're here, I'd love a tour of Truelove's main attractions."

In his humble but accurate opinion, right now the woman sitting beside him was the best thing Truelove had going for it.

"The Mason Jar." He pointed. "City hall has the fire department, paramedics and the police, too." He veered around the square. "There's the library."

Hunter looked up from the game. "There's my school, AnnaBef."

She snuggled against his son. "Looks like you have fun there."

"With my best fwend, Maisie. Over dere." He

gestured toward the gazebo on the green. "I told Santa I didn't want any toys for Chwistmas. Just a mommy."

And so it began… The awkward conversation he'd been trying to avoid since they first met.

The look she sent Jonas's way could've peeled paint off a house. Hunter returned to the game.

Maybe if Jonas made out like it wasn't a big deal, he could head her off at the pass.

"Funny, huh?" He dared not look in her direction. "And you were the next woman we ran across." He forced a laugh. "Literally, almost ran across."

But AnnaBeth didn't laugh.

Wincing, he pulled into the auto-repair-shop lot. Zach had the sports car docked in the open bay of the garage.

Somehow, despite the height difference, she managed to look down her nose at Jonas. "I'm sure any female would have fit the bill."

He'd never met anyone who did haughty as well as she did.

"That didn't come out right." He sneaked a look at her face. "It was the bow on your head. The fancy dress. You looked gift-wrapped."

Hunter glanced up. "The best Chwistmas pwesent ever, AnnaBef." His eyes shone. "I want you to be my mommy more dan anyone else in de world."

Knuckles white on the wheel, Jonas held his breath. *Please, please don't crush him...*

"I love you, too, Hunter." Her eyes shimmered. "Nobody's ever wanted me more than anyone else in the world," she whispered.

Jonas fell against the seat. He could see how she'd feel that way after that Scott dude jilted her. He could relate. He had his own abandonment issues.

She hadn't said much about her family. But surely that didn't apply to them? What about her father?

"Wook, Dad!" Hunter leaned forward. "Zach is waving for us to come inside." In a flash, he undid the buckle, threw open the door and hopped out.

"I've tried telling him, but he won't listen to me." Jonas scrubbed his face with his hand. "He thinks God sent you to us special because he wished for you on Santa's lap."

She slid toward the open door. "Via a broken-down sports car and a snowstorm."

"I'm sorry. I never meant to put you in this position."

"What choices have you left me with, Jonas?" Stepping out, she slung her purse strap over her shoulder. "Tell him the truth and destroy his child-like faith or what?"

Getting out of the truck, he laid his hands palms flat on the roof of the cab. "I don't know. I'll talk

to him again." He blew out a breath. "But don'
worry. I won't let him hold you hostage. I'm sure
you want to get back to your own family as soon
as possible."

"You'd be surprised what I wish for, Jonas."
She threw him an unreadable look. "And I don'
believe with God there are coincidences."

He swallowed. "I don't, either."

"So what's your Christmas wish, Jonas?"

"I—I didn't... I don't wish for anything."

Striding toward the building, she tossed her hair
over her shoulder. "Maybe that's your problem
Perhaps you should."

After what happened at the pond, he was convinced God had sent AnnaBeth to them. *But only
to save their lives, right, God?* Yet his heart did
an odd sort of twisty thing in his chest. For something more, too?

Just his loneliness talking. He slammed the
door. The truck rocked.

He had God. He had his family. He had the
ranch. Everything he ever wanted or needed
Until...

Jonas watched AnnaBeth introduce her bubbly
never-met-a-stranger self to Zach. In his blue me-
chanic coveralls, his cousin wiped the grease from
his hands before shaking hands with AnnaBeth.

Even from a distance, he could tell Zach was
fairly dazzled.

Clenching his jaw, Jonas wandered inside the
ay. Hunter had found a convenient tire on which
o perch and continue his game.

Zach bobbed his head. "Jonas, my man."

He stuck his hands in his pockets. "Thanks for
etrieving her car, Zach. What's the verdict?"

Whistling long and low, Zach pushed his ball
ap higher onto his forehead. "She's a real beauty."

An unpleasant feeling knotted his gut. Jonas
cowled. "Her name is—"

"The car." Eyes widening, Zach swept his arm
oward the sports car. "Never saw one of these
n person before. Much less had a chance to get
under the hood."

He and Zach leaned over the engine while his
ousin pointed out the issues.

AnnaBeth shifted nervously. "So what does that
ctually mean?"

Straightening, Zach closed the hood of the
ports car. "It means I've got good news and bad
ews. Which do you want first?"

"Definitely the good news first."

Jonas gave her a cockeyed glance. "Really?"

She nodded. "The good news will help me
ear the bad news better. As long as there's hope,
here's life, right?"

He wasn't sure how to respond to that.

"Why would you want bad news first?" She
lted her head, looking at him with those big

green eyes of hers. "Once you hear the bad, it'
hard to appreciate anything good."

She had a point. He'd always considered him
self a realist, but in light of her soaring optimisr
that things had to get better, perhaps he was mor
of a pessimist than he realized.

He squared his shoulders. "Okay, good new
first then."

She sucked in a breath. "What did you just dc
Jonas Stone?"

His gaze darted from his cousin to AnnaBetl
"Nothing…"

"Yes, you did. You were bracing, weren't you?
She poked her finger in his chest, punctuating he
words. "Bracing for good news. Seriously?"

Zach appeared as dumbfounded as Jonas felt.

She threw out her hands. "What kind of perso
braces for good news? Are you always waiting fo
the other shoe to drop?"

"Maybe." He thrust out his jaw. "Maybe I am.

"But that's such a sad way to live."

He guessed it sort of was. He didn't used to b
like that. Just since Kasey.

Brow creasing, Zach looked from AnnaBeth t
him. "Are you two done now?"

She laughed. "For now."

Jonas forced a smile. "So tell us this great—
he flicked his eyes at AnnaBeth to make sur

she was paying attention "—wonderful. Fabulous. Good news."

She smirked. "That's the spirit."

Zach rolled his eyes. "The good news is that I can fix your car so you can be on your way again."

Rising on the balls of her feet, she clapped her hands. "Oh, thank you, Zach."

Didn't sound like good news to Jonas.

"And the bad news?" he growled.

Zach scratched his head. "I'm going to have to special-order a part. It could take a few days."

Midclap, AnnaBeth came down on her heels. "Oh."

Not such bad news. In fact, the best news Jonas had heard in months. Years.

"Keep us updated." Chest broadening, he found himself smiling. "But do whatever you have to do, Zach, ol' buddy." He clapped his cousin across the shoulder blades. "I suppose we'll just have to make the best of it."

She glinted her eyes at him.

And since they were in town…

Suddenly, Jonas had a great idea. He hummed the opening line to "It's Beginning to Look a Lot Like Christmas."

Perhaps this Christmas might not be so terrible after all.

Chapter Ten

That evening, Hunter hung his favorite Christmas ornament—a ceramic cowboy—on the tree. "It's de biggest twee ever."

It *was* big. Huge. At least a twelve-footer and it still didn't come close to brushing the top of the vaulted ceiling.

She placed an ornament with Hunter's baby picture on a higher branch. The pungent aroma of cedar and pine filled the lodge.

Unlike the professional decorators Victoria brought into their Charlotte home every year, the FieldStone-Ranch tree was a family project.

At dinner, ErmaJean's chicken-and-rice soup had been delicious. Deirdre had declared she was already feeling better. But she'd soon excused herself to wrap some gifts, leaving the tree decorating in their capable hands.

Smiling, AnnaBeth stepped back to survey

their efforts. It was beginning to look a lot like Christmas at the FieldStone.

Adorned with red tartan ribbons and tiny, colorful silk birds, the tree complemented the rustic decor of the lodge. But in her opinion, the Field-Stone tree was every bit as beautiful as Victoria's Christmas-on-steroids version.

"'Deck the haws wif boughs of ha-wee,'" Hunter sang, getting into the spirit of the holidays.

Speaking of Christmas spirit, she didn't know what had gotten into Jonas Stone.

Out of the corner of her eye, she watched him wrap the fragrant pine garland around the staircase banister. And would wonders never cease? He was humming under his breath as he worked.

After leaving Zach's shop and stopping by the pharmacy, he'd insisted they head to a nearby Christmas-tree farm, owned by one of his friends. Unlike Charlotte, everyone in the greater Truelove area apparently knew everybody else.

"'Fa-wa-wa-wa-wa—'" Hunter threw open his arms, caroling at the top of his lungs "'—wa-wa-wa-wa!'"

Biting back a laugh, she caught Jonas's gaze. His lips twitched.

She lifted her chin. "''Tis the season to be jolly,'" she sang.

"Who wants to help put bows on the presents

for me?" Deirdre called, leaning over the upstairs railing.

"Me!" Hunter shouted and raced for the stairs.

Deidre smiled at them, waiting for Hunter to join her. "Somebody's happy."

And he wasn't the only one.

Though how Hunter would feel when her unexpected winter ranch vacation was over, she preferred not to contemplate. Lately, the FieldStone felt far more real than her life in Charlotte.

If she even had another life or family to go back to. But another Victoria maxim—no sense in letting the uncertainty of the future cloud the sunshine of today. She'd enjoy Hunter, Deirdre and the ranch as long as she could. Jonas, too.

She flicked her gaze to the man himself, who was hanging a garland across the massive stone fireplace. The familiar, melted-butter feeling quivered in her belly.

Who was she kidding? She sighed. She'd enjoy her time with Jonas, most of all.

Later that night in her room, AnnaBeth finally found the courage to read Victoria's messages. *What's happened? Why did you leave? What did Scott do? Why didn't you come to me?*

AnnaBeth and her stepmother staged houses together. They went shopping together. They planned parties together. But talk? Victoria did the talking, and she usually did the listening.

Frowning, she reread the text. Not what she'd expected. She'd figured Victoria would immediately blame her. She pulled up the next one. *Are you all right??? Where are you? Please. Talk to me.*

She bit her lip. Victoria actually sounded worried. She'd have thought her stepmother would rejoice to be rid of her.

AnnaBeth scrolled through the rest of the texts, now numbering in the teens. More of the same. Growing increasingly frantic. At some point over the last couple of days, MaryDru and Scott had apparently told Victoria about their feelings for each other. *Please, AnnaBeth. Don't shut me out. We can work this out with your father. Call me. I need to know you're okay.*

Guilt nibbled at AnnaBeth's conscience. No text from her father, but Victoria had long been his mouthpiece. She hadn't been fair to him. He must be worried about her. And when he was stressed, he fell into unhealthy habits.

But she wasn't ready for a confrontation with Victoria. Still… Before she changed her mind, she speed-dialed MaryDru.

Her sister picked up on the first ring. "Anna-Beth? Is that you?"

"It's me," she whispered.

MaryDru sucked in a breath. "Oh, A.B. I'm so, so sorry. We've been going crazy, not knowing where you are. Mom's done nothing but cry."

The knife twisted in her gut. She'd never seen Victoria cry about anything. Crying made wrinkles.

"But Scott told you I was okay, right?"

"He told me what you s-said…" Her voice broke into a sob.

Fresh guilt assaulted AnnaBeth. Her baby sister sounded as if she'd been crying for a long time.

"I meant what I told Scott, MaryDru. I want you two to be free to love each other. Really. It would make me happy to see you happy."

"Please come home, A.B." Her sister dissolved into tears. "Mom and I need you. Things aren't good here with Dad."

Her heart tore. She couldn't stand this distance between her and her sister. Emotional and physical.

But already, the FieldStone felt more like home than Victoria's house ever had.

She fretted the zipper on her puffy vest. "I-I'm not ready to leave the FieldStone Ranch yet, MaryDru."

If she had her druthers, she'd never leave. But when had AnnaBeth's wishes ever mattered to her family? To anyone?

She bit her lip. "I've got to go now, sis."

"No! A.B., wait."

"I—I have to go, MaryDru."

"But you'll be home for Christmas, won't you, A.B.?"

"I don't know, MaryDru. I can't make that promise. I just need more time to…"

To what?

She swallowed the lump in her throat. "Tell Victoria I'm fine. I'll call you soon." She clicked off before once again she allowed herself to be swept away by her sister's need.

But this time… This time she refused to disregard her feelings.

For the FieldStone. For Hunter. For his father and how he made her feel. Made her feel about herself.

The next morning, because snow still blocked remote area roads, Hunter's preschool was closed for another day.

AnnaBeth shook her head. "I didn't realize it got more remote than this." She gestured toward the window overlooking the meadow.

Headed outside, Jonas snagged his hat off the peg. "Hate to break it to you, but the FieldStone's off one of the main mountain roads, darlin'."

As soon as the words left his lips, his face flamed.

They stared at each other across the kitchen.

Had he said what she thought he said? She mustn't have heard him right. Had he called her *darlin'*?

Mouth in a thin, straight line, he clamped his hat on his head and stalked out the door.

"Well, now…"

She jumped. She'd forgotten about Deirdre.

Deirdre smiled over the rim of her coffee cup. "Aunt IdaLee will be so pleased at this turn of events."

"I'm sure I don't know what you mean." Anna-Beth took her seat at the breakfast table. "It was nothing more than a slip of the tongue."

Deirdre laughed. "A Freudian slip."

Perched on the edge of the chair, she steepled her hands on the table. "Jonas and I might be friends, Deirdre. But I don't think he *like*-likes me."

His mother's eyes rounded. "Why ever do you think that?"

She dropped her gaze. "He frowns at me a lot. Most of the time, in fact, he glares at me. And scowls."

"That's exactly what makes me think he does *like*-like you, AnnaBeth."

AnnaBeth's eyes snapped to hers. "That doesn't make any sense."

"Welcome to the world of men, and most particularly my son, honeybun."

She pleated her napkin into folds. "Jonas thinks I'm a spoiled, empty-headed rich girl."

Deirdre reached across the table and placed her hand over AnnaBeth's, halting her restless plucking of the napkin. "Honeybun, it's because he doesn't—can't—allow himself to smile at you that makes me believe he definitely likes you. Very much, in fact."

AnnaBeth worried her lower lip with her teeth. "He told me about what happened between him and Hunter's mother."

Deirdre's smile faded. "Kasey hurt him badly. They wanted different things out of life. He's afraid to let himself feel anything for fear of getting hurt again." Her eyes lit up. "But I'm so glad he shared that with you. He doesn't tell many people. He obviously trusts you."

"I saw the photo of Hunter's mother." AnnaBeth lifted her chin. "So gorgeous. So capable. So thin." She swallowed. "So blond."

Deirdre picked up her coffee cup. "Seems to me Jonas prefers redheads."

"Prefers… Oh." AnnaBeth fingered a dangling tendril of her hair. "You think so?"

Deirdre took a sip. "I think so."

AnnaBeth insisted on washing the breakfast dishes. When a thud hit the floorboard overhead, they both glanced at the ceiling.

Deirdre smiled. "Hunter's awake."

Coming downstairs in his cute cowboy pjs, he was thrilled to learn his snow vacation had been extended another day. After he'd eaten and dressed, he wanted AnnaBeth to read him *The Snowy Day* again. Deirdre headed to the laundry room to do a load of wash.

Later, after AnnaBeth closed the book, Hunter bounced up, eager to go outside. "We haven't built our snow people yet."

AnnaBeth inched out of the chair. "We can't have that, now, can we?" She gestured. "Get your boots and coat."

Stopping outside the laundry room, she realized Deirdre was on her mobile phone. Anna-Beth bit back a sigh. The infamous Aunt IdaLee or Dwight?

Which reminded her she needed to call Mary-Dru again tonight. And find out how things were going with Scott. She didn't need their breakup on her conscience, too.

Making hand motions, she mouthed to Deirdre that they'd be outside. Smiling, Hunter's grandmother waved her off.

By the time she donned her winter gear, Hunter was out on the terrace throwing a rope over the plastic steer dummy.

His face brightened when he saw her. "I pwactice ev-wee day." He pushed up the brim of his hat with the tip of his finger. "I'm going to win."

She took his earnest little face between her mittens. "I know you will." Only she wouldn't be here to see it. "Let's make some snow people, what do you say?"

"Hoo-way!" He jumped off the terrace and made for a mound of snow Jonas had shoveled into a large pile. "Watch me swide down the mountain, AnnaBef. Wheeeee!"

They spent the next hour packing handfuls of snow between their gloves and rolling them into small, medium and larger balls.

"Cwunch. Cwunch. Cwunch." Hunter stomped his feet. "I'm walking wike Peter in de book."

She laughed. They created four snowmen of varying sizes. Running over to the edge of the woods, Hunter scoured the ground for branches to make sticklike arms.

Returning, he dragged his feet, slowly making tracks. "Wike Peter."

AnnaBeth's heart swelled with an almost maternal pride. He really was the most adorable, sweetest little boy she'd ever known. And so smart.

He stuck a carrot for a nose in the smallest snow person. "Does de snow wook wike dis where you wiv, AnnaBef?"

Unwinding the scarf from her neck, she draped it around the medium-size snow person. "We never get this much snow, and what we get doesn't stay pretty long with all the cars and people."

"Looks like you two have been busy."

She whirled. Drat her heart.

A smile on his hunky features, Jonas stood, arms folded across his coat, under a gigantic evergreen tree.

"I didn't hear you come up." She put her hand to her throat in a vain attempt to quiet the rocketing of her pulse. "We were having so much fun."

He cocked his head, the Stetson at an angle. "So much fun, you never missed me?"

She narrowed her eyes, not sure she was properly interpreting the question she saw in his dark gaze.

Hunter brandished one of the sticks he'd gathered. "Of course, we missed you, Dad."

Jonas looked at her. "What about you? Did *you* miss me?"

She'd never before appreciated how thin the air must be here in the mountains. Why else was she having such a hard time breathing?

"When you're not around, Jonas, I always miss you."

Her heart drummed in her chest. She'd said it. Actually told him what she was feeling. She didn't know whether to faint from horror or sigh with relief.

One corner of his mouth curved. Then, the other side. A slow, sweet, buckle-your-knees smile. Just for her.

"Thank you." His voice had gone all gravelly. "I like spending time with you, too."

Could Deirdre possibly be right?

She felt like doing a little dance in the snow. Singing a song. Sheer bliss.

Jonas surveyed their handiwork. "What's this, Hunt?"

Like a barker at a carnival displaying his wares, Hunter swept the stick through the air. "It's us, Dad." He pointed to the tallest snowman. "You."

Deirdre had supplied them with an old cowboy hat and other accessories.

Hunter gestured at the next snow person. "Gwam-ma."

Jonas scratched his cheek. "Sunglasses?"

Hunter bobbed his head. "'Cause Gwam-ma is cool."

Jonas laughed. "That she is."

"Dat's me." The smallest snowman also sported a cowboy hat and a red bandanna. A coil of rope hung from one of the stick arms.

AnnaBeth made a sweeping motion toward her scarf-draped snow self. "And me." She batted her eyelashes. "See the resemblance?"

"I'm not seeing it." He shook his head. "Where's the mouth?"

Marching over, she punched him in the arm. "Hey!"

Jonas grinned.

"You guys awe so si-wee." Hunter poked the evergreen with his stick. With a plop, a patch of snow fell on AnnaBeth's head.

She screamed.

Jonas laughed.

She brushed the snow out of her eyes. "Don't make me hurt you." Then she laughed, too.

"I fink I'm weady to go into de warm house wike Peter."

Jonas's stomach growled. "And eat."

She took one of Hunter's hands. Jonas took the other. It felt nice walking toward the house. Like they belonged together.

Like a real family?

She reckoned she really must be silly. *Stop day-dreaming, AnnaBeth.* Jonas Stone was way out of her league.

But it was a lot of fun to daydream. No harm in dreaming.

Was there?

She sat Hunter on a stool in the mudroom. "We need to get these wet socks off."

His son let out a happy sigh. "Just wike Peter."

Jonas toed out of his boots. "Looks like I need to read this book if I hope to have a conversation with either one of you ever again."

His mother wandered into the kitchen. "I got an email saying preschool is back in session tomorrow. Your snow vacation is over. And I saw those lovely snow people you created, sweetie."

He looked up proudly. "My snow famiwee, Gwam-ma."

Jonas's gut knotted. Hunter was getting too attached to AnnaBeth. Every day she appeared more and more comfortable on the ranch. She fit so well into their lives. They were all getting too attached.

His mother's cough had gotten better, but AnnaBeth insisted on being in charge of dinner. "As long as I'm here, consider yourself on vacation from the kitchen."

"I'm never gonna want you to leave." His mother smiled. "If you're not careful, I could get used to this."

His heart pricked. So could he. And elaborate, completely delusional scenarios of what it would be like if AnnaBeth stuck around dogged his thoughts the rest of the afternoon.

Only later that evening did he realize he'd never heard from Zach.

AnnaBeth perked, her eyes lighting up. "I have a great idea."

Those eyes of hers… Green, his new favorite color.

"What's your great idea?" he rasped.

"Christmas cookies." She looked from him to his son. "What do you think?"

"Hoo-way!" A human pogo stick, Hunter bobbed in his stocking feet. "I wuv Chwistmas cookies! Can I help?"

"Of course. Who else? You're the best little cowboy helper I've ever had."

Jonas's heart constricted. The way she was with his son… It felled him every time.

AnnaBeth headed for the pantry. "Victoria and I make these every year."

Hunter hopped on the counter stool. "Do you eat them all?"

She deposited the flour and baking powder on the counter. "Only a few. Victoria, my sister and I take the rest to the oncology ward at the hospital."

His mother tilted her head. "That's so nice. Why the oncology ward?"

AnnaBeth stopped, midmotion. "I never thought about it before. The only person I know who had cancer was…" She blinked. "My mother."

"That's very sweet for your stepmother to make that gesture."

A line puckered AnnaBeth's forehead. "I—I guess so."

His mother moved toward the backstairs. "Call me old-fashioned, I need to finish this year's Christmas cards. But I'll look forward to eating a few Christmas cookies at breakfast."

Jonas hadn't failed to notice his mother had

been doing a lot of that lately—leaving him, AnnaBeth and Hunter alone.

He needed to tackle some paperwork, and hadn't meant to get involved in the baking, but the laughter between his son and the lovely runaway bride soon drew him in.

Jonas couldn't think of another place he'd rather be—watching them roll cookie dough and dust each other with flour. He couldn't take his eyes off AnnaBeth and Hunter.

He didn't want to miss a single moment.

Chapter Eleven

Filling the coffeemaker with water Wednesday morning, AnnaBeth glanced through the window to see Jonas headed toward the house. Hard at work as usual, it appeared that he'd already been to the barn.

She poured the water as he entered the house. "Good morning."

Toeing out of his work boots, his head snapped up. "Morning." He shrugged out of his coat and hung it on the peg in the mudroom. "I didn't see you there."

His voice had a raspy, unused quality first thing in the morning. She attributed the high color in his cheekbones to the frosty morning.

She measured out the grounds. "You look like you could use some coffee."

"That would be great, thank you." His gaze darted. "Where's Mom?"

"It was my turn to put breakfast on the table." AnnaBeth got the coffee percolating and then took out the skillet. "Can I fix you some eggs?"

He removed several mugs from the cabinet. "I can make do with cereal."

Pursing her lips, she tightened her hold on the iron frying pan. "You work hard, and you need something substantial to tide you over until lunch."

His eyebrows rose.

She placed her other hand on her hip. "It's not often I get the chance to cook, so how about letting somebody do something for you for a change?"

His mouth snapped open and shut.

She brandished the skillet. "Why can't you just say 'Why thank you, AnnaBeth. Breakfast would be lovely.'" She glared at him. "Unless you're afraid I'll poison you. Is that it, Jonas? You're afraid I'm going to poison you?"

He cocked his head. "Why, thank you, AnnaBeth." He gave her the slow, slightly crooked smile that made her knees go weak. "Breakfast would be lovely." He pulled out a chair, sat down and looked at her.

Just looked at her.

"You're not planning on hitting me over the head with that, are you, AnnaBeth?"

"Not right now." She lifted her chin. "But the day's still young."

He laughed.

With a clang, she set the skillet on the stovetop. "Fried or scrambled?"

"I'll have what you're having."

"I'm not—" She pressed her lips together. "Scrambled then. Maybe Hunter would like some, too." She looked at the clock on the wall. "Should I make sure he's awake?"

Jonas scooted out of the chair. "I'll go get him dressed."

"Give me ten minutes, and I'll have breakfast ready."

"Thanks." He fingered the stubble on his jaw. "Maybe after breakfast you'd ride into town with me. After we drop Hunter off at school, we can check with Zach about how the repairs are going and how soon he expects to have you on your way."

Was he hoping she left sooner versus later?

She was putting the finishing touches on the last plate of eggs when Hunter tromped into the kitchen.

Grabbing her around the legs, he gave her an exuberant hug. "AnnaBef!"

His father trailed after him, carrying a child-size backpack. "Gramma's going to stay here and take it easy this morning."

AnnaBeth helped Hunter climb into his seat at the table. "Maybe I should stay here and—"

"But I want you to see my classwoom."

Jonas held out AnnaBeth's chair. She smiled at him and sat down.

A cowboy and a gentleman... Be still my heart.

Taking a seat, Jonas said grace and then wasted no time digging into breakfast. Making sure Hunter had a firm grip on the juice glass, she watched Jonas for his reaction to her culinary effort.

"Are the eggs okay? Would you rather I—"

"The eggs are delicious. Thank you."

She angled toward Hunter. "Maybe he would prefer his eggs fried?" She started to rise.

Jonas put his hand over hers as Hunter shoveled another forkful into his mouth. "I think he likes them just fine, don't you, Hunt?"

"Yummy." In between bites, Hunter nodded. "Dank you, AnnaBef."

"You are very welcome, sweet boy."

Jonas sipped his coffee. "You said you didn't cook often. Why's that?"

"I like to cook, but we had Mrs. Salisbury. She didn't like MaryDru and I to be in the kitchen."

He cocked his head. "You had a professional cook in residence?"

"Nobody ever crossed Mrs. Salisbury. I think even Victoria was afraid of her." She smiled. "But I like eating here much better than our huge dining room. Cozier. Nicer."

Then their cozy, nice beginning to the day

ended. There was a mad scramble to get Hunter
into proper winter gear. She scurried around getting the kitchen to rights.

But AnnaBeth was at her best when taking care
of other people. She loved nothing better. And as
the rays of the sun climbed ever higher over the
mountain ridge, there was an added bonus. Going
to town meant spending more time in the company of Jonas.

AnnaBeth, this isn't going to end well for you.

Buttoning Hunter's coat, Jonas gave her that
lovely lopsided smile of his. Her heart fluttered.

For the love of sweet potatoes, get a grip.

"Ready, AnnaBeth?"

She smiled, switching off the doubts in her
head. "I'm ready, Jonas," she said.

Every day, a little more of the snow melted. But,
aware of the threat of black ice, Jonas was cautious driving into town. The truck clanked over
the bridge spanning the river. They passed the
Welcome-to-Truelove sign.

"'Where true love awaits...'" AnnaBeth said,
reading aloud. "Huh."

He rolled his eyes. "Exactly."

"I guess it's back to business as usual."

His mouth curved. "This is what passes for rush
hour in Truelove." He turned his head. "Unlike

he morning traffic you're used to in Charlotte,
'm sure."

"It's nice. Truelove is charming."

He grimaced. "That's cause you've only been
here five minutes."

"You don't fool me, Jonas Stone. You love this
little mountain town, and you know it."

He grinned. "Yeah, you've got me there. I guess
I do."

Problem was, Kasey hadn't. And probably no
one else—like AnnaBeth—would be content to
live here, either.

Despite his idle daydreaming, what would a so-
phisticated city girl like AnnaBeth do in a backwater place like Truelove?

AnnaBeth scanned the shops on Main Street.
"I'm not sure how in the world I ended up on the
mountain instead of in town."

Jonas turned into the preschool parking lot off
the town square.

Hunter hugged her arm. "God knew we needed
you, AnnaBef."

Thing was, she was beginning to suspect it was
actually the other way around. It was she who
needed them.

She got out of the truck and helped Hunter put
on his backpack. He'd insisted on wearing his
cowboy hat. Hunter had also looped a small coil

of rope around one of the straps of the backpack Apparently, a must-have cowboy accessory.

So, so cute.

An idea for a future post? Except she'd title it Must-Have Accessories for the Well-Dressed Cowgirl.

Jonas patted his shoulder. "Are you glad to be back at school, Hunt?"

"I guess." Hunter squared his jaw. "But I don' want de sunshine to melt awe de snow. 'Cause der AnnaBef might go away."

"But AnnaBeth's going to have to—" Lips thinning, Jonas ushered them into the building.

She threw him a glance. The moody cowboy was back. He'd seemed so lighthearted in the truck. But just as quickly, he'd reverted to his usual, closed-off, gruff self.

Frankly, she was beginning to get whiplash trying to keep up with his changing moods.

Jonas walked his son and AnnaBeth into the classroom.

"You're here." A bubbly little girl with curly blond hair ran over and gave Hunter a hug.

"Dis is my best fwend in de world, AnnaBef." Solemn as a parson, Hunter stuck his thumbs in his belt loops. "Dis is Maisie."

And like the proper lady she was, AnnaBeth

held out her hand to the little girl. "I am so pleased to make your acquaintance, Miss Maisie."

Jonas spotted Maisie's dad working his way around the preschoolers toward them.

"AnnaBeth, this is Jake McAbee, Maisie's father. His family owns the Apple Valley Orchard." Jonas clapped his hand on his shoulder. "Jake, this is AnnaBeth Cummings. She's staying at the lodge."

"Pleased to meet you." The sandy-blond-haired orchard grower extended his hand. "I didn't realize the FieldStone took guests this time of year."

She shook his hand. "Hunter and Jonas found me stranded on the side of the road during the snowstorm and took pity on me."

"More like she took pity on us." Jonas smiled. "Mom's under the weather. AnnaBeth's been pitching in at the ranch with Hunter and chores."

"I'm sorry to hear about your mom, Jonas. Callie will probably insist on bringing y'all a pie."

The tenderness in Jake's eyes when he said his wife's name caught Jonas square in the chest. A sharp, lonely feeling. Always on the outside of love, never on the inside.

Saying goodbye, Maisie's father departed. At Hunter's insistence, AnnaBeth met his preschool teacher and most of his classmates before Jonas succeeded in pulling her away.

Next stop—Zach's auto-repair shop.

She sailed into the garage ahead of Jonas. "Hopefully, good news. Fingers crossed."

But instead of relief at the prospect of sending her on her way at long last, a strange feeling of impending doom came over him.

Zach emerged from the office, wiping his greasy hands on a cloth. "Cuz. Miss AnnaBeth."

Jonas's eyes narrowed. "Zach." Was it his imagination, or was his cousin avoiding eye contact?

Gaze plastered to the concrete, Zach stuffed the rag into his pocket. "What can I do for you folks today?"

"You can tell us when you estimate you'll have AnnaBeth's car repaired."

"About that?" Zach made a face. "There's been an unforeseen delay with the order."

She frowned. "What kind of delay?"

Jonas folded his arms. "You ordered the part when we saw you on Monday, didn't you?"

Zach scraped his hand over his mouth. "Well, you see, after you left, Miss GeorgeAnne stopped by..."

Jonas jutted his jaw. "What's that got to do with anything?"

"She said she was hearing a funny noise in her truck engine. Insisted I take a look. Spent a good hour—"

"Did you order the part or not, Zach?"

"I meant to, Jonas, but I got distracted. And then after she left—"

"Spill it, cousin."

Zach spread his arms wide. "I couldn't find the paperwork I'd written up with the parts number. I looked and looked, but then Aunt IdaLee called." He gave AnnaBeth a sheepish look. "She had dinner on the table and wanted me to come straight over. I don't get home-cooked meals often."

AnnaBeth nodded. "So, of course, you had to go."

Zach's shoulders relaxed. "She was counting on me."

"*We* were counting on you," he growled.

And to his thinking, it was no coincidence GeorgeAnne Allen had been on the premises when the paperwork did a vanishing act.

"You hated to disappoint her," AnnaBeth said, in that soothing voice of hers.

"Thank you, AnnaBeth." Zach sniffed. "I'm glad some people still have a heart."

"What's your excuse for not placing the order on Tuesday, cousin?"

Zach rubbed his neck. "Monday night Aunt Ida-Lee made it clear. It's you or me, cuz," he mumbled.

Jonas glared. "What's that supposed to mean?"

Zach's eyebrows rose. "I think you and I both know what that means."

"Stop gnashing your teeth at him, Jonas." She laid a hand on his arm. "I'm sure Zach will re-write the paperwork this morning and get the part ordered first thing."

Jonas made an elaborate show of looking at his watch. "It's going on ten o'clock. So much for first thing. What are we looking at, Zach?" He planted his hands on his hips. "Another two days?"

Zach pushed out his lips. "Three at the most."

"Not like we have any choice, do we, since you're the only repair shop in town?" He made a noise in the back of his throat. "I absolutely can-not believe you, Zach. I can't believe *them*."

Zach shuffled his feet. "I'll try to overnight the part, if it'll make you happy. But don't you dare let on."

He jabbed his index finger at his cousin. "I'll tell you what would make me happy..."

She tugged at his arm. "Coffee would make me happy. And possibly one of those apple-cider doughnuts Hunter told me about might sweeten your disposition, too."

He allowed himself to be towed from the ga-rage. "This is exactly what I feared from the be-ginning."

She ignored him. "A short walk will do you good."

Leaving the truck parked, he stalked across the

green toward the Mason Jar. "I knew they were brazen, but I had no idea they'd stoop to this."

He slowed his pace when he realized he was practically dragging her alongside him.

"They who?" She slipped her hand through the crook of his arm. "Stoop to what?"

What hadn't escaped his attention this morning was how pretty she looked in the soft-as-a-cloud, lavender sweater. Even to his untrained eye, he recognized the fabric as an expensive cashmere.

"We've been sabotaged, AnnaBeth." He reached for the handle on the café door. "On an industrial scale. The matchmakers have conspired with Zach to keep you from leaving town."

He threw open the door for her. The overhead bell jangled.

She let go of his arm. "Maybe I shouldn't have suggested we come here, Jonas. I'm so sorry for embarrassing you. You'd probably prefer not to be seen with me."

The door whooshed shut behind them.

"It's me who's embarrassed." Finding her hand, he laced his fingers in hers. "We must look like a bunch of backward hicks to you."

Only gradually did he become aware the crowded diner had gone silent. Raising his head, he found himself staring straight into the gazes of the three matchmakers at their usual table. Dropping her hand, he went rigid.

"Not them," he groaned. "Anybody but them."

Following the track of Jonas's gaze across the diner, AnnaBeth noted the three old women seated at a table on the far wall near a bulletin board.

Recognizing ErmaJean, she surmised these women must be the matchmakers that had half the town—the male half, at least—running scared.

But no one liked to be railroaded. She should know. AnnaBeth glanced at Jonas. And no one liked to be forced to do something they didn't want to do.

Why was everyone staring? So quiet she could've heard a pin drop, she felt her cheeks heat. She took a quick, indrawn breath. What would Victoria have done in this situation?

Suddenly, though, AnnaBeth knew. "Let me handle this."

"Wh-what?" he stammered.

"A good offense is the best defense." She brushed her hair off her shoulders. "I've got this."

AnnaBeth sailed across the diner toward the matchmakers. Leaving Jonas to flee, or follow in her wake.

She wouldn't have blamed him if he'd fled. But he was made of sterner stuff. She should've known he'd have her back. He was a cowboy, after all.

When they spotted her headed their way, the old women's eyes appeared about to pop out of their sockets.

AnnaBeth widened her smile. "Ladies." She steepled her hands underneath her chin. "I can't tell y'all how de-lighted I am to finally make your acquaintance."

ErmaJean recovered first. AnnaBeth wasn't surprised. She'd been told ErmaJean was the most talkative.

The twins' grandmother nodded at her matchmaking compatriots. "*This* is AnnaBeth, ladies."

Seriously? As if the other two didn't already know her name? These women had no idea whom they were dealing with.

AnnaBeth laughed, injecting a merry note into her voice. "And I am so purr-fectly de-lighted to meet y'all."

She flicked her eyes at Jonas. *Too much?* But he winked. Her smile broadened.

"Jonas has told me so-o-o much about you. Such dears, you are."

The women gaped.

She smiled hugely at the angular, faintly terrifying woman with the ice-blue eyes and short, iron-gray hair. "Miss GeorgeAnne."

"AnnaBeth." GeorgeAnne the Formidable har rumphed. "A double name, like us."

Hands clasped to her bosom, she batted he eyes at the oldest and most diminutive membe of the trio. "And you must be Jonas's great-aunt IdaLee."

Jonas's eyes ping-ponged from his aunt tc AnnaBeth.

"Do you think I could join your double-nam club? Maybe I can also become an honorary matchmaker in Truelove." She struck a dramatic pose. "Where true love awaits."

GeorgeAnne's eyes got squinty. ErmaJean opened her mouth, but AnnaBeth beat her to the punch.

"I understand you three are also single." Beam ing at them, AnnaBeth clapped her hands together "I simply can't wait to help you ladies find you perfect match, too."

Silverware clanged. Customers gasped. The Truelove Matchmakers appeared speechless.

"Shots fired," choked Jonas.

AnnaBeth fluttered her lashes at GeorgeAnne "I've got my eye on a certain judge for you." She swung toward IdaLee. "How do you feel abou insurance salesmen?" AnnaBeth tapped her fin ger on her chin. "But I'm saving a retired schoo administrator for you, Miss ErmaJean."

ErmaJean sputtered.

"Alas, dear ones." She glanced at her wrist-watch. "I've no time to share my plans for your personal love connections with you today, but perhaps another time. Soon." Twisting her lips, she gave them the I-mean-business look. "Count on it."

Jonas bit back a strangled laugh. They'd better get out of here before he lost it.

AnnaBeth snagged hold of his coat. "Have yourselves a wonderful day now, ladies, you hear?"

Waggling her fingers at the matchmakers, she couldn't be certain, but she thought she saw Ida-Lee's lips twitch.

They no sooner exited the diner than Jonas collapsed against an SUV in the parking lot. "I can't believe you…"

Sudden doubts assailed her.

Yet doubled over with his hands on his knees, tears of merriment leaked out of his eyes. "The look on their faces…"

Had she made a perfect fool of herself in front of the whole town?

"Was it too over-the-top?"

"About time somebody turned the tables on those scheming seniors." He swiped his hand across his eyes. "AnnaBeth Cummings, you are the most amazing woman I've ever met."

It may have been her imagination, but she

thought she detected something besides admiration in his eyes.

All at once, she didn't care if her car ever got fixed. Not if it meant she'd have to leave this cowboy behind.

Chapter Twelve

Thursday morning, Christmas songs blared from the small radio on a workbench in the bay of Zach's garage.

Jonas scowled at his cousin. "Let me get this straight. You still don't have the part for Anna-Beth's car?"

Zach met his gaze head-on. "This time it isn't my fault, Jonas."

"Forgive me if I have trouble believing you, Zach." He shook his head. "You told me you were going to overnight it."

"And I did." His cousin folded his arms. "But AnnaBeth's special-delivery part wasn't on the freight truck with the other packages. I don't know what happened."

Jonas scrubbed his neck. "Oh, I have a pretty good idea exactly what happened." He stalked outside and threw himself into the truck.

As he passed the hardware store, he considered confronting GeorgeAnne, but instead he gunned the motor and decided to save time by tackling the real mastermind behind Operation Christmas Mommy.

Veering into the quiet neighborhood off Main, he pulled to a stop beside IdaLee's turn-of-the-century Victorian home. He strode across the broad, gray-planked wraparound porch, and knocked on the wreath-bedecked door.

The seconds ticked by.

"Aunt IdaLee," he shouted. "I know you're in there 'cause you don't drive when there's snow on the ground."

He pounded his fist on the door, setting the wreath a-quiver. "I'm not going anywhere until you open this door, Aunt IdaLee. I want to talk to you."

There was a shuffling sound on the other side before IdaLee threw open the door. "I'm coming, I'm coming. Don't get your spurs in a twist. I don't move as fast as I used to, you know."

Rocking on his heels, he glowered at his great-aunt.

"What has you in such a dither, nephew?" Smirking, she patted her snow-white hair. "Or should I ask, who?"

"Don't play innocent with me, Aunt IdaLee."

She gave him that teacher look she'd used to

her advantage for decades. "What, pray tell, are you accusing me of now?"

"You know what you did. You and your partners in crime are up to your doilies in this."

"Crime? What crime?" She sniffed. "I have no idea what you're talking about."

Jonas's cell phone buzzed in his pocket.

"This is the last straw, Aunt IdaLee. You've gone too far. Mail theft happens to be a federal crime."

He ignored the continuing buzz from his cell.

"Mail theft?" Her bright blue eyes blinked at him. "You think I've stolen someone's mail? What mail?"

The relentless buzzing stopped.

"Packages are mail, Aunt IdaLee. AnnaBeth would be within her rights to press charges. You—or more likely some former student—hijacked the special-delivery part for AnnaBeth's car right off the truck."

"Is that what this caterwauling is about?" His very proper, maiden aunt rolled her eyes. "I have no idea what happened to the package, but neither I nor any of the other matchmakers had anything to do with it, I assure you."

Like a persistent mosquito, the cell buzzed again.

"You better come inside before we both get pneumonia." IdaLee's blue-veined hand tugged him into the old-fashioned foyer. "And for the love of sweet tea, answer that phone."

She shut the door behind them as he dug the cell out of his pocket. A text from Zach. *Driver found package. Accidentally delivered to wrong address.*

He scrubbed his hand over his face.

IdaLee directed a pointed look at his hat. "From your expression, I'm guessing the lost package has been located?"

Sheepish, he nodded. And took off his hat.

"All's well that ends well."

"That doesn't excuse everything else you've done, Aunt IdaLee."

"I'm sure I have no idea what you're referring to, nephew."

He gritted his teeth. "I'm talking about how you blackmailed Zach into aiding and abetting your schemes."

IdaLee's mouth turned prim. "Blackmail is such a harsh term."

He narrowed his eyes. "Blackmail is such an accurate term."

She studied him for a long moment. Long enough for Jonas to squirm.

"Have no fear, dear heart." She squeezed his arm. "The good Lord will work everything out for the best."

Jonas clenched his jaw. "Did it ever occur

to you ladies that the good Lord doesn't need your help?"

"Of course, He doesn't need our help. What do you take us for?" She spread her hands. "We had nothing to do with the storm. The blizzard was an act of God."

These old women were going to be the death of him.

His elderly aunt's wrinkled face softened. "Even when you were Hunter's age, you were always so serious. And later you became the strong, silent type." Her cheeks sagged. "Not always a good thing, especially when you were hurting."

Jonas tried swallowing past the lump in his throat.

"But you can't live the rest of your life afraid of getting hurt by love again, dear boy."

Hadn't AnnaBeth said something similar?

IdaLee smoothed down the corner of his upturned collar. "I like that runaway bride of yours."

"She's not my—"

"I admit we've had to take some unusual and unprecedented measures to keep her from resuming her road trip. To give you both sufficient time to grasp the possibilities." IdaLee's eyes glinted. "You've been our hardest case yet. But we're determined to see you happy, Jonas, even if it kills us."

"Or me," he grunted.

She smiled. "How hard you make it on yourself, my stubborn nephew, is entirely up to you.'

Was happiness possible for someone like him?

IdaLee glanced at the grandmother clock on the wall. "Aren't you supposed to pick Hunter up from preschool about now?"

He'd lost track of time. Between the matchmakers, his son's mommy wish and AnnaBeth, he might be in danger of losing his mind.

Smelling of lavender, IdaLee caught him in a hug. "Don't forget how much your old aunt loves you, Jonas."

Despite never having children of her own, every Christmas she'd had a gift for each of her nieces and nephews. She always managed to get him what he wanted most.

Though sometimes he didn't know it was what he most wanted until he unwrapped her gift on Christmas Eve.

He returned her hug. "I won't, Aunt IdaLee." His Adam's apple bobbed. "And you're not old. You'll outlive us all."

Pulling away, her blue eyes twinkled. "Clean living." She wagged her gnarled finger. "Let that be a lesson to you. You hear?"

"Yes, ma'am." He blew out a breath.

Back in the truck, he headed toward Hunter's school. Why was he fighting the matchmakers so hard? If you can't beat 'em, join 'em.

Why not enjoy Christmas this year? Why not enjoy this brief interlude of happiness with AnnaBeth?

But for Jonas, happiness had proven as elusive as morning mist on the mountain.

And as he gripped the wheel, he couldn't help but wonder how much reaching for happiness might cost him this time.

With Hunter at school Friday morning, Deirdre and AnnaBeth decided to take a short road trip. About an hour's drive from Truelove, Asheville was a fun, quirky city.

Deirdre had asked for AnnaBeth's advice in updating the worn decor in the FieldStone cabins. AnnaBeth was only too thrilled to help.

They shopped. They ate lunch in a trendy café near Pack Square. They shopped some more.

And they talked. She found herself telling Deirdre things she hadn't intended to reveal. Or realized about herself. Her self-doubt. Her insecurities.

Including what happened the day of her wedding.

Later that afternoon, they decided to stop at a tearoom near Biltmore Village before returning to Truelove. It was a lovely, cozy shop. Each dining area had a different-themed Christmas tree.

Amidst the clinking of china, she told Deirdre about her parents and their divorce.

"You were living with your mother when she died?"

"I was not much older than Hunter." AnnaBeth nodded. "Everything from that time is blurry, but I remember feeling lost. And alone." She glanced out the tearoom window at the passing cars. "I still do."

She remembered a bitter, cold day at a cemetery. Her mother's friends and coworkers had gathered. A pastor spoke words over her mother's coffin.

AnnaBeth had searched the crowd in vain for the face that mattered—her father's. Yet at some point that day, he must've arrived, although she couldn't recall the exact details. When he came to bring her home to live with him.

Her only other tangible memory that day was of a woman holding tightly to her hand. And the beautiful, velvet bows on the woman's to-die-for, high-heeled shoes.

"My fascination with footwear started young."

Deirdre reached across the tea table, wresting AnnaBeth from the sadness of that long-ago day. "You remind me of a parable Jesus told his disciples."

AnnaBeth blinked. "I remind you of a parable?"

"The pearl of great price." Deirdre smiled. "The

story is about a merchant seeking exquisite pearls. And when he found one, he sold everything he had to purchase it."

AnnaBeth took a sip of tea. "Still not sure I know what you mean."

"There are several interpretations of the story, but here's the one that reminds me of you."

AnnaBeth placed her cup in the saucer.

"Jesus is like the merchant, searching and seeking precious ones to make His own. And the price He paid for His bride, the church, was His life."

AnnaBeth knotted the napkin in her lap.

"You, AnnaBeth, are one of those pearls."

Tears sprang to AnnaBeth's eyes. "I—I never thought of the story that way." Her mouth quivered. "Or myself that way."

"You should, because that's how God sees you."

Finding the Bible app on her phone, Deirdre pointed AnnaBeth to other Scriptures passages.

"Lost sheep. Lost coin." AnnaBeth swiped a finger under her eye. "Is it me, or are you sensing a pattern?"

Deirdre's mouth quirked.

"I wish my stepmother had been someone like you, Deirdre." She grimaced. "Instead, I got the queen of mean. Tennis lessons. Ballet. Etiquette classes. Cotillion. The debutante ball. I could go on."

Deirdre drew her eyebrows together. "Was she

truly mean to you, AnnaBeth? Or trying to broaden your horizons? Make you the best you could be?"

AnnaBeth sniffed. "She was trying and failing to make me as perfect as her."

Deirdre ran the tip of her finger around the gold rim of the cup. "How exhausting."

AnnaBeth rolled her eyes. "Tell me about it."

"I meant your stepmother, Victoria." Deirdre leaned forward. "I can't imagine how frustrating and hopeless she must feel. Always trying to live up to some impossible ideal. Trying to please others when the only one we should strive to please is God."

AnnaBeth made a face. "That's Victoria."

"Last last bit? I was talking about you, honeybun."

AnnaBeth glanced up, but Deirdre's eyes were kind.

"God made you just as you are, AnnaBeth. Gorgeous, capable—"

"Not thin, though."

Deirdre placed her hand over AnnaBeth's. "God made you, AnnaBeth Cummings, just right."

"But not blond."

"God made you a beautiful, loving, vivacious redhead. You must learn to love yourself." Deirdre squeezed her hand. "Because you're wonderful. God doesn't make junk."

"Except for the junk in my trunk?"

"I'm being serious here."

AnnaBeth smiled. "I know. And I love you for what you said. I promise I will think about those bible verses."

Soon after, they resumed their journey back to the FieldStone. But the day wasn't finished surprising AnnaBeth.

When they arrived at the lodge, Jonas was in the midst of planning a surprise of his own.

A light dusting of snow fell on Saturday morning. AnnaBeth had feared the snow might derail the bonfire Jonas had organized for his friends that night in the meadow underneath the stars.

But as she was learning, mountain folk were intrepid. They weren't willing to let a little precipitation stand in the way of a good time.

Whereas, Charlotte would have ground to a complete halt at the first snowflake.

The snow gave the ranch a renewed beauty. Hunter gathered sticks to roast marshmallows. Jonas had bought graham crackers and chocolate bars to create s'mores. The crisp chill in the air was a perfect companion to the welcome warmth of the fire.

Jonas had talked a lot about his friends. He'd invited those closest to him to the FieldStone, making it something of an occasion.

Frankly, she was nervous. These people meant

a lot to him. Would they like her? Then she recalled one of the verses she was trying to commit to memory.

"I must please God, not men. Please God, not men," she whispered.

"What?" Jonas joined her near the edge of light cast by the fire.

"Nothing," she muttered.

Keeping an eye on Hunter, who was jabbing a stick in a snowdrift, they awaited the arrival of Jonas's guests. Deirdre and Dwight had opted for a "real" date at the Jar. A public declaration they were officially a couple.

Headlights gleamed, rounding the curve in the long driveway.

"Callie and Jake," Jonas said.

AnnaBeth had already met everyone but Callie. Amber and Callie were best friends. Their husbands had extended their friendship to Jonas. She prayed they'd expand the circle to include her as well.

Voices floated across the distance. Hunter's head snapped up. "It's Maisie!" He dropped the stick. "Maisie! Maisie!"

He raced toward the little girl with the bouncing blond curls as fast as his boots would carry him.

Waving, the little girl ran to meet him. "Hunter! Hunter!"

AnnaBeth cut her eyes at Jonas. "Put them in slow mo—give or take a few decades—and you've got an epic blockbuster love story there, my friend."

Jonas stuck his tongue in his cheek. "You're referring to one of those chick flicks, aren't you?"

She gave him a saucy grin. "Nothing wrong with a little romance."

"Nothing at all." The flickering flames cast his chiseled features in sharp relief. "How about after this crowd leaves and we get Hunter to bed, you find that epic love story on Netflix?"

"It's a date." She choked. "I—I mean—"

"You were right the first time." He brushed his finger across her cheek. "It is a date." Then he walked away to greet Callie and Jake.

Grateful the darkness hid the crimson in her cheeks, AnnaBeth headed over to join them and Jonas introduced her to Callie.

Ignoring the adults, Hunter and Maisie caught up on the events of their lives since last they met—yesterday at school.

Jake shook his head. "Dear old dad doesn't exist once Hunter Stone comes along."

Callie hugged her husband's arm. "As much as Maisie loves her daddy, I don't think you need fear losing your baby girl just yet." She winked at AnnaBeth. "But like her mama, she does have right good taste in men."

AnnaBeth laughed. "Who doesn't love a cowboy?"

Doors slammed from another vehicle. Callie and her husband moved to greet the Green family.

Turning on her heel, AnnaBeth plowed straight

into a solid mountain of a man. And she found herself, nose-to-chest, with Jonas himself.

"Who doesn't love a cowboy?" Jonas caught hold of her elbows. "Is that so? Are you speaking from personal experience, flatlander?"

She dragged her gaze from the steady beat of the pulse in his throat to his liquid brown eyes. "Uh-huh…"

Jonas wrapped a strand of her hair around his finger. "I'll hide the marshmallows. You hide the chocolate." Leaning closer, he whispered into her ear. "Then maybe everyone will go home. And we can have that movie date."

Her hunky cowboy smiled. AnnaBeth felt like floating skyward alongside the sparks from the fire.

But the bonfire proved fun, too. She enjoyed Jonas's friends. She appreciated how Amber and Callie went out of their way to get to know her. Turned out, they were *Heart's Home* readers, too.

After a lovely evening, eventually everyone went home. And she did find a chick flick on a cable channel. She and Jonas stayed up late, talking. Laughing. Getting to know each other.

Getting better acquainted with each other's hearts.

And despite the lack of sleep, she got out of bed the next morning before the first rays of sun topped the ridge. Sunsets were spectacular here, but there was just something about sunrise and the start of a new day, bright with possibilities.

She still hadn't summoned the courage to deal with Victoria, but every night she called Mary-Dru. AnnaBeth felt confident her sister and Scott were making progress toward a lasting future together. She tried not to dwell on the fact she had yet to hear from her father.

Like most families on Sunday morning, it was a mad scramble to get to church on time. She fell in love with the two-hundred-year-old sanctuary, the wide-planked beams soaring overhead and the prisms of light shining through the stained-glass windows.

She loved the hymns. The reading of God's word. But most of all, she loved the sense of shared faith. The community of fellow believers.

After church, Jonas's mother and Dwight decided to do some Christmas shopping at an outlet mall on the highway. And Jonas left AnnaBeth in the sanctuary while he handed Hunter into the care of the McAbees. Little Maisie was hosting a children's Christmas party at the orchard that afternoon.

AnnaBeth was so busy admiring the hand-crafted altar she failed to notice the matchmakers advancing on her until it was too late. She soon found herself surrounded.

"My, my, IdaLee," GeorgeAnne clucked. "The

way that nephew of yours looks at this here red-headed gal."

AnnaBeth blushed.

Tiny IdaLee plumped her lips. "Every time she walks into a room, he has eyes only for her."

ErmaJean clapped her age-spotted hands together. "That's a song. Isn't that a song, GeorgeAnne?"

If nothing else, these ladies were tenacious. She'd been foolish to imagine the matchmakers had dropped their campaign. Only a strategic retreat until they could regroup.

Miss IdaLee lifted her chin. "And I've seen how you look at him, missy, when you think no one is paying attention."

"I may be old, but I'm not too old to remember giving my dear departed husband a look like that myself when we were a-courting." ErmaJean patted her shoulder. "Are you and Jonas courting now, dear?"

She gulped. Were they? She thought about last night.

About how they'd laughed. How happy she'd been. How happy Jonas had seemed. As if the years and the cares of the world had vanished from his face.

"I suppose." She took a steadying breath. "Maybe we are."

GeorgeAnne pushed her glasses higher on the bridge of her nose. "Excellent."

IdaLee nodded. "I thought as much."

ErmaJean smiled. "How wonderful."

And round two went to the matchmakers.

Riding back to the lodge with AnnaBeth, Jonas decided he wouldn't mind more alone time with their snow princess.

When they arrived, he came around and opened the truck door for her. Gathering the folds of her black velvet skirt, she eased out of the truck. Such a girly-girl.

Jonas didn't know much about clothes, but he knew enough to know he liked what he saw. The tall black leather boots. The fancy green winter coat. But most of all, AnnaBeth herself.

Her sweet spirit. Her shining eyes. And her hair... He went weak-kneed every time he thought about her hair.

Last night at the bonfire before everyone converged on them, he'd plucked up the courage to satisfy his curiosity. Wrapping a tendril around his finger, her hair was as he'd supposed. Red silk.

He bit his lip. "AnnaBeth..."

She gave him a bright smile. "Yes, Jonas?"

"Uh..." He pushed the brim of his hat higher on his forehead, then scuffed his boot in the snow. "Um..."

"I know it's hard." She batted her lashes. "But it's important to use your words, sweetheart."

Smirking, he scooped up a snowball. "I prefer action to words."

"Jonas Stone…" Her eyes enlarged. "Don't you dare…" Then she ran.

Laughing, he chased her across the lawn.

Coming to an abrupt halt, she held up her hand. "Stop right there, cowboy."

He hefted the snowball. "Why?"

She gave him a look. "Because it's not polite to chase people."

Lunging, he grabbed hold of her coat collar. Yanking her close, he held her back against his chest.

"Jonas!" Trying to prevent him from putting the snowball down her back, she wriggled. "Jonas!" she squealed.

"I'm not chasing you, flatlander," he rasped in her ear. "I've caught you."

As graceful as a ballerina, she turned in his arms. She looked at him with those tremulous green eyes of hers.

"Yes," she whispered. "You've caught me."

He dropped the snowball. It landed with a soft thud on the snow-packed ground.

And suddenly, he had the feeling it might be the other way around. That she had caught him.

She felt so good in his arms. So right. Like she'd

always belonged. And nothing that had gone before mattered.

If only he'd known he had but to wait for a
snowstorm—or his son's Christmas wish—to
bring AnnaBeth to him.

She turned her face to his. "Oh, Jonas."

He cradled her face in his palms. "Would it
be okay, AnnaBeth—" he reminded himself to
breathe "—if I…?"

"Yes, Jonas." Stretching on her toes, she wound
her arms around his neck. "Please do."

He brushed his lips across her mouth. And
when she didn't pull away, he deepened the kiss.
She was more than he'd allowed himself to dream.

Sweet. Good. Someone, who'd never betray
him.

His breath fluttered the strand of hair dangling
near her earlobe. "Wow."

"Fireworks." She smiled at him. "Does this
mean you *like*-like me, Jonas?"

Jonas laughed. "Yes, I think it definitely means
I *like*-like you."

"Good." She grinned. "Because I *like*-like you,
too."

"Marvelous," he murmured.

She lifted the hat off his head, then resettled it
upon hers. "What do you think? How do I look?"
She crinkled her eyes at him.

"We'll make a cowgirl out of you yet. You look

good, flatlander." He pulled her close. "Good enough to kiss."

And then he did.

Chapter Thirteen

Monday morning, AnnaBeth offered to take Hunter to school. "I need to pick up a few things while I'm in town."

Jonas threaded his fingers through her hand. "Like what?"

"It's Christmas." She kissed his cheek. "This time of year, cowboys should know better than to ask too many questions."

While he worked to repair the porch handrail, his mother also left for town and then returned with Aunt IdaLee.

Holding on to his great-aunt's arm, his mother made sure IdaLee didn't lose her footing coming up the walk.

IdaLee stopped to talk to him. "Ran into your runaway bride while we were in town."

His mother smiled. "She sure looked happy.

Nearly as happy as you when Dwight brought me back to the ranch yesterday."

Jonas didn't say anything. He had it on good authority cowboys didn't kiss and tell.

"For the love of sweet tea, Jonas." His aunt wagged a bony finger at him. "I hope you're not going to do something stupid and lose that girl. Besides your son, she's the best thing that ever happened to you."

"Yep." He nodded. "She's a keeper."

"And what's more—" IdaLee peered at him. "What did you say?"

He cocked his head. "I agree with you. AnnaBeth is a keeper. And that's exactly what I intend to do—keep her."

IdaLee's head reared back a fraction. "Well," she harrumphed. "Glad to see you've finally come to your senses."

His mother bit off a smile. "Let's get you in the house, Aunt IdaLee, and see about some of that applesauce cake I promised."

Jonas returned to his repairs. With the help of a buddy, Zach had delivered AnnaBeth's car to the ranch Sunday afternoon. But after all that had happened between them, she looked in no hurry to leave the FieldStone.

They'd discussed attending the tree lighting on the town square together later that week. And the parent/student Christmas party at Hunter's school

He wasn't clear on the details yet, but he felt
sure somehow he could convince her to put off
her departure indefinitely.

Jonas was putting the final screw in the handrail when a sleek, blue BMW rolled through the
gateposts and parked in front of the lodge.

A woman in her late forties jumped out of the
car. Small, rail-thin with delicate pixie features,
she had big brown eyes and sleek short, brown
hair. Her jewelry looked expensive.

He reckoned her brown high-heeled boots alone
probably cost more than a month of groceries. An
ominous feeling roiled his gut.

"Where's my daughter?" Heels clattering on
the sidewalk, she rushed over to him. "What have
you done with her?"

Sudden fear assailed him. The repercussions
of this woman's arrival had the potential to shake
AnnaBeth to her core. And he felt helpless to do
anything to stop it from happening.

"I have the county sheriff on speed-dial." The
petite woman brandished her cell phone in his
face. "I demand to see AnnaBeth immediately."

After finishing her shopping, AnnaBeth drove
back toward the ranch. She and Hunter sang
Christmas carols all the way up the mountain.

He gave the sports car an admiring pat. "I wike
your caw."

She steered carefully around the winding road. "I'm thinking of trading it in for something more practical. Like an SUV." A smile spread across her face. "Better for ranch living."

Truth was, she'd been so giddy last night she'd barely gotten five hours of sleep. And when she did sleep, her dreams were full of a certain hunky cowboy…and a little cowboy, too.

Pulling through the gateposts at the FieldStone, she reflected she'd never imagined she could be this happy.

May your heart always find its way home.

For the first time in her life, she believed she finally had. Her life was here on the FieldStone.

And though nothing had yet been said between them, in his eyes she saw the words he wasn't yet able to say.

Not yet, but soon. She knew it in her heart. Soon, together they'd establish the family they'd each always dreamed of.

At the lodge, as she pulled alongside a familiar BMW, foreboding needled her chest.

Gentleman in the making, Hunter helped her tote her Christmas purchases. But reluctance dogged her steps.

Jonas met them at the door. "There's someone here to see you, AnnaBeth."

Sinking dread gripped her belly.

Ushering them inside, he squeezed her hand before they entered the living room. In a red car-

ligan twinset and wool skirt, IdaLee sat on one
nd of the sofa as prim as the teacher she'd once
een. On the other end of the couch, Deirdre lifted
troubled face to AnnaBeth.

Her stepmother rose from AnnaBeth's favorite
hair. In less time than it took to blink, they sur-
eyed each other.

Victoria had tucked her winter white jeans into
er favorite Italian boots. The big, clunky gold
ecklace glistened at the neck of her oversized
Aran sweater, a garment that emphasized her stepmother's tiny frame.

When AnnaBeth found the courage to lift her
gaze to Victoria's face, what she beheld there took
er breath. She saw regret and a pain so deep AnnaBeth had to look away.

Hand outstretched, Victoria took a step toward
er. "Bethy…"

AnnaBeth scowled. "How did you find me?"

"MaryDru." Dropping her hand, she pinched
er lips together. "Please, don't be angry with her.
begged her to tell me."

Then AnnaBeth recalled letting the name of the
anch slip during one of her conversations with
MaryDru.

Jonas rested his hand on the small of her back.
Comforting. Protective.

The gesture did not go unnoticed by her stepmother.

Deirdre cleared her throat. "Aunt IdaLee has

been telling Mrs. Cummings about the Doubl
Name Club."

The silence grew uncomfortable between th
adults, but, aware of none of it, Hunter sidesteppe
his father and AnnaBeth.

Arms laden with shopping bags, he peere
from under the brim of his hat at Victoria. "Is di
your mommy, AnnaBef?"

"Victoria is my stepmother." Using him not un
like a human shield, she placed her hands on hi
shoulders. "Not my mother."

Her stepmother flinched.

Deirdre got off the couch. "AnnaBeth, don't.'

"Hunter?" IdaLee inched her way upright
"Why don't you put the shopping bags in Anna
Beth's room?"

Sharp, blue eyes missing nothing, the ol
woman looked from Victoria to AnnaBeth. "
don't know about the rest of you, but Hunter an
I are ready for lunch."

By mutual agreement, they tabled anythin
other than polite conversation for later.

Hunter and Jonas disappeared upstairs, and th
unlikely quartet of women headed into the kitche
to make lunch.

For the last nine days, AnnaBeth had bee
given the run of the kitchen. She and Deirdr
had become a well-oiled team at putting food o
the table.

When she took out a paring knife to slice a to-mato, Victoria rushed to her side. "Let me help you with that, Bethy." She gave AnnaBeth a wob-ly smile. "Like old times."

"No, thanks. Deirdre and I have everything under control."

"Oh." Victoria's eyes darted between them. "Of course. I see. I'll just sit down over there out of your way, then."

Lips tightening, Deirdre threw AnnaBeth a hard look.

IdaLee cleared her throat. "My parents were the first to open the ranch to guests. They of-fered meals to the young men working on the nearby Blue Ridge Parkway during Roosevelt's New Deal."

"Hospitality and heritage are important." Bit-ing her lip, Victoria looked through the bay win-ow to the snow-covered ridge. "This is a special place. I'm so happy Bethy found her way here."

Not trusting herself to speak, AnnaBeth con-centrated on not slicing off a finger.

Lunch wasn't as awkward as she'd feared. Vic-toria was a master at the niceties of polite conver-sation and putting others at ease. From time to time, Jonas touched AnnaBeth's hand under the table. Yet, surprisingly, Hunter took to her step-mother right away.

After lunch, he insisted on taking Victoria onto

the terrace to show her the correct way to rope
steer. She appeared genuinely delighted to spen
time with the little cowboy. Like AnnaBeth, Vic
toria had always been good with children.

Finally, though, AnnaBeth could put off th
hard conversation with her stepmother no longe

She wanted Victoria to leave. She wanted onl
to be surrounded by people who loved her. Here
the FieldStone, where she felt herself on the brin
of becoming the AnnaBeth that God always in
tended for her to be.

"You should probably go soon, Victoria. It
best to get off the mountain before dark."

Her stepmother fingered her keys. "Would yo
walk me to the car?"

AnnaBeth nodded.

"Thank you for your hospitality, Deirdre." Vic
toria's dark eyes gleamed. "And for listening."

Deirdre hugged her. "You're always welcom
at the FieldStone, Victoria."

IdaLee patted Victoria's arm. "You did wel
dear heart. AnnaBeth does you credit. She's suc
a jewel."

AnnaBeth kept her thoughts on that one to her
self.

Victoria hugged Hunter. She extended her han
to Jonas. "Thank you for taking such good car
of my daughter."

He dipped his head. "It's been our pleasure, Mrs. Cummings."

Walking out of the lodge, AnnaBeth and her stepmother were silent. The snow crunched under their feet. They stopped beside the BMW.

"You're not ever coming home, are you?" Victoria rasped.

AnnaBeth shook her head.

Victoria hugged her arms around her sweater. "I think MaryDru and Scott are going to work things out between them."

"All I ever wanted was for MaryDru to have her chance for happiness."

Victoria swallowed. "I know you won't believe me, but that's all I ever wanted for both my girls."

AnnaBeth clamped her lips together to keep them from trembling.

"I never would've pushed you and Scott to marry if I'd known you truly didn't love him." Victoria's thin shoulders rose and fell. A helpless, hopeless gesture. "I knew he would treat you the way you deserved. He's a good guy."

"Scott is a wonderful guy."

Had Victoria always looked so fragile? Or was AnnaBeth only now noticing?

"But more importantly, Bethy, I knew Scott would love you for who you are."

"Only as a friend, though." AnnaBeth sniffed. "And that kind of love isn't enough, Victoria."

"No." She turned away, her gaze roaming ove the snowy landscape. "You're right. It isn't."

An uncomfortable suspicion gripped Anna Beth. Had Victoria been trying just as despe ately to "earn" Hayes Cummings's love as h daughter?

Perhaps she and Victoria had more in commc than she'd known.

AnnaBeth crossed her arms. "Why did yo come here, Victoria?"

"Just like before. The first time." Her step mother bit her lip. "I had to make sure my Beth was all right."

"I'm not your…" AnnaBeth took a breath. "I' left messages on Daddy's phone, but I haven heard from him. Do you think he'll ever forgiv me? Is he still so very, very angry with me?"

"Your father—" Lips parting, she appeare about to say something, and then changed he mind. "I met your father only a month after h divorce."

Wait. After the divorce? She'd always assumed–

"I'm making some changes in my life, Anna Beth. Necessary changes, a long time comin But I want you to know that no matter what hap pens, wherever I am, my home will always b your home."

"What do you mean 'wherever you are'?" A naBeth's voice rose. "Where are you going?"

Resignation clouded Victoria's flawless features. AnnaBeth realized that her eyes were almost the exact shade of brown as Jonas's eyes.

"I'm sorry for pushing you so hard. For failing you. For never being enough." Victoria winced. "For not being the mother you wanted."

What was going on here? It sounded as if Victoria was saying goodbye. Forever.

She touched AnnaBeth's face. Not the first time she'd tried to do that. But the first time that AnnaBeth let her.

"MaryDru might've grown under my heart." Her palm cradled AnnaBeth's cheek. "But from the moment I laid eyes on you, Bethy, you grew in it."

Before she could think of how to respond, Victoria got into the car. Annabeth stood there until the red taillights of her stepmother's vehicle disappeared over the incline in the drive.

Jonas, Hunter and IdaLee came out of the house.

"Hunt and I are taking Aunt IdaLee home." His forehead creased. "Are you okay?"

She tucked her hair behind her ear. "I'm fine."

He gave her a meaningful look. "You sure?"

She managed a weak smile. "No, really. I mean it. I'm fine." With her finger, she smoothed the line on his forehead. "No need to scowl, cowboy. Just hurry back, okay?"

He adjusted the angle of his hat. "Will do."

Seeing Victoria had left her feeling oddly unsettled. And difficult conversations appeared to be on the menu today.

Inside the house, feet flat on the floor, Deirdre's fingers tapped the armrest of the couch. She didn't look happy. "Victoria told me about your father. And his drinking problem."

Sinking into the armchair, AnnaBeth made a face. "She shouldn't have told you about him. That's never mattered to me."

"Running away will never solve your problems, honeybun. Unless you face the broken relationships in your past, how can you hope to create a new life for yourself?"

"It isn't Daddy's fault. It's Victoria. She never—"

"Victoria might not have been the mother you wanted, AnnaBeth." Deirdre raised her chin. "But Victoria was the mother you got. The mother God knew you needed. God doesn't make mistakes."

AnnaBeth shook her head.

"Her mothering may have sometimes been misguided over the years, but Victoria loves you, AnnaBeth. Yes, she made mistakes. But she did the best for you that she knew how." Deirdre's eyes flashed. "As do most mothers for their children. As one day, you'll discover for yourself. You're very like her. Did you know that?"

AnnaBeth recoiled. "I'm nothing like her."

"You have her elegance. Her incredible sense of style and grace." Deirdre gestured. "You view the world through the same lens. Like it or not, for better or worse, good and bad, we are more like our mothers than perhaps we care to admit."

AnnaBeth blinked rapidly.

"But most of all, what I see of her in you, Anna-Beth, is the overwhelming sweetness my son could no more resist than a bee to honey."

AnnaBeth squeezed her eyes shut. "I—I don't want to talk about this anymore, Deirdre."

Getting off the sofa, Deirdre wrapped her arms around AnnaBeth. "I don't say these things because I want to hurt you. I love you, honeybun."

AnnaBeth's throat clogged with unshed tears.

"But no ranch, no child, no spouse, no human being will ever be able to fill the hole that's inside you. Only God can fill that kind of emptiness. And He will, if you ask Him to."

There was truth in her words that resonated deep within AnnaBeth.

She hugged this dear woman of God. "It's not only Hunter and Jonas that I thank God for bringing into my life."

AnnaBeth didn't sleep much that night. When she finally did fall asleep, she dreamed she was a little girl again. At her mother's funeral.

Lost and alone, she seemed to be chasing something or someone, always just out of her reach.

She awoke crying, confused and unsure about what had been real memories and what hadn't been.

A nagging uncertainty plagued her—the sense that she'd overlooked a vital piece of information. Something Victoria said…

Yet, unable to puzzle it out, she spent the morning wrapping her Christmas presents for the family. Deirdre was busy in the kitchen. With Hunter at preschool, Jonas was out and about somewhere on the ranch.

She was arranging the gifts under the tree when she realized she'd misplaced her phone.

AnnaBeth wandered into the kitchen. "By any chance, did I leave my phone in here?"

Perched on an island stool, Deirdre pored over her grocery list. "'Fraid I haven't seen it, honey-bun."

"Huh…" Chewing the inside of her cheek, she cast her mind about for the last place she'd set it down.

"Maybe you left it in Jonas's truck earlier. When you two carried Hunt to preschool?"

AnnaBeth snapped her fingers. "That's it. You're a genius."

Deirdre laughed.

AnnaBeth tied a scarf around her neck and

ventured outside. But there she discovered Jonas standing by the open door of his truck. Her cell phone sat in his hand.

She hurried over. "You found it."

When he looked up, he wasn't smiling. "I heard ringing. When I picked it up, I couldn't help but see the name of the caller."

AnnaBeth held out her hand. "No problem. I'll ring them back. I hope it wasn't something important."

Eyes narrowed, he handed her the phone. "You tell me."

She frowned. "What's wrong, Jonas?"

He looked away. "I wasn't aware you and your ex-fiancé were still in contact."

"Oh, that."

His gaze returned to hers. "Yeah, that." His face shadowed. "Do you still have feelings for him, AnnaBeth?"

"No, Jonas." Without meaning to, she'd hurt him. "It's not that at all."

"Then what?"

She was shaken by the raw vulnerability in his eyes. Loving someone was a privilege. A sacred responsibility.

In that moment, she realized she loved Jonas. Deeply. With all her heart.

But secrets didn't make for happily-ever-afters.

AnnaBeth moistened her lips. "There are still issues Scott and I need to resolve, Jonas."

Setting his jaw, he stuck his hands in his pockets.

AnnaBeth caught his arm. "I promise it's not what you think."

His Adam's apple bobbed. "I don't know what to think."

She needed to come clean with him about her wedding. But it was almost time to pick up Hunter.

"This afternoon, maybe you and I could go for a drive. Alone. Can you wait 'til then? I promise I'll tell you everything, Jonas. Please?"

He probed her features. Trust was his biggest issue. She held her breath. She'd do anything not to lose his trust in her.

Jonas kissed her forehead. "'Til then."

She let the breath she'd been holding trickle through her lips. "Thank you, Jonas."

"You want to ride to town with me to pick up Hunter?" Jonas rubbed his chin. "He'd rather see your pretty face than this old cowboy mug of mine. Not that I blame him."

She smiled. "Let me grab my coat."

They walked into the house together. She was about to take her coat off the peg when her cell phone rang in her hand.

Without checking caller ID, she clicked on. "Hello?"

"AnnaBeth."

"Daddy?" Her mouth went dry. "Is that you?"

Her father had finally called. She'd been so worried. She held up her finger for Jonas to give her a minute.

"We've got time," he whispered as he detoured to pour himself a cup of coffee. Deirdre gave her a thumbs-up.

She turned back to the phone. "Daddy, it's so good to hear your voice."

"Hello, sweetheart. I'm so sorry I haven't returned your calls sooner."

Sweetheart… She gulped.

AnnaBeth could count the number of times he'd called her sweetheart and still not use all the fingers of her hand. She went limp with relief. Did this mean he'd forgiven her? That he wasn't going to shut her out of his life forever?

In the background on the other end, she heard someone paging a doctor.

"Daddy?" She gripped the phone. "Where are you?"

Her eyes flitted toward Deirdre and Jonas. Jonas made a motion as if to leave and give her some privacy. But she gestured for him and his mother to stay. She had a feeling when she got off the phone, she might need their support.

"Daddy, what's wrong?"

"I've done something I should've done a long

time ago. I've checked into a treatment center, AnnaBeth."

Victoria had been after him so long to make changes in his life. To get help. Counseling. But he'd always refused.

And when the stress of life got to be too much, he fell off the wagon. Time and time again.

She sank into a chair at the kitchen table. "Are you okay, Daddy?"

Her father took a shuddering breath. "Not yet, but I will be. I've made such a mess of everything. Now I've lost her. Lost my family. Lost you."

Lost *her* who? Victoria?

"You haven't lost me, Daddy," she whispered into the phone. "I'm glad you're getting help."

"When Victoria got home yesterday, we had a long talk. A long-overdue conversation. She told me I had to get help or—" His voice hitched. "I've hurt all of you so m-much."

Had Victoria left her father?

"I'm so ashamed. I let my anger toward your mother overshadow our relationship."

She rubbed her forehead. "I don't know what you mean, Daddy."

"Victoria's convinced she'll never see you again. It's breaking her heart, AnnaBeth."

She closed her eyes. "Daddy—"

"That's the reason I'm calling. You deserve the truth about that day. A truth that does me no credit, but its time for me to make amends before our family completely fractures."

Her heart pounded. "What are you talking about, Daddy? What day?" She quivered.

Suddenly, she was afraid. Afraid to hear what he had to say. She had a bad feeling the next few minutes would irrevocably alter her life.

"Daddy, it's okay. I love you. You don't have to tell me any—"

"Sh-she wouldn't l-leave you. I told her that l-life was a m-mistake. B-better left in the past."

Wait. He was talking about her. Had AnnaBeth been the mistake he'd wanted to leave behind?

"Please f-forgive m-me, AnnaBeth. I'm so sorry for not being there when your mother died. I'm so sorry for not being there for you since," he sobbed.

Tears flooded her eyes. She'd never heard her father cry before. Hearing the brokenness in him, she felt helpless.

And responsible.

Running away had set a chain of events in motion. With far-reaching consequences she'd never intended. Despite the picture-perfect image, theirs was a family only one slight breeze away from falling apart.

"Despite everything, I do love you. I'm sorry I've done such a poor job showing you how much."

Not a man to offer affection, he'd never told her he loved her before. Hearing the words was like a balm to a wound that had long festered, but never fully healed.

Yet the moment was bittersweet. She had to fix this. Fix everything.

"This is my fault, Daddy." Her breath came in short, painful gasps. "I should've never walked away from Scott. If I'd stayed—"

"The blame lies with me. But I've realized only God can fix this. Fix me."

She closed her eyes. "Daddy, you don't need to say anything else."

Please, please, don't say anything else.

"I wouldn't go to your mother's funeral. But Victoria went. And afterward, she refused to release you to Social Services."

The memories from that terrible, lonely day crystallized. Stabbing her heart like shards of glass. Her father hadn't been there. He hadn't come.

And her world, as she'd known it, rocked. Including everything she'd believed about herself.

"But I promise you, sweetheart, whatever it takes, I'm going to become the father you and MaryDru deserve. The man I should've been." His voice became strangled. "I don't deserve your forgiveness. But please don't blame Victoria. None of this was ever her fault."

Unable to continue, he broke the connection,

leaving her stunned. Floundering. Grappling with something she'd never suspected.

She recalled Victoria's words yesterday. About how she'd come looking for AnnaBeth before… The pieces of the puzzle fell into place as the day of her mother's funeral took on a new clarity.

Like a lens shifting into focus, everything clicked into place. It wasn't her father who'd brought her home to live with him. Dropping the cell onto the table, she slumped forward.

"AnnaBeth, what's wrong?" Deirdre's voice sharpened.

"The shoes… Why didn't I realize?" Tears sprang into her eyes. "The shoes with the beautiful velvet bows."

Deirdre wrapped her arms around AnnaBeth's shaking shoulders. She'd been unwanted by her own father. Unloved.

"It wasn't Daddy who insisted Victoria take me into their home and raise me." She bit back a sob. "It was Victoria who refused to leave me in foster care."

Deirdre sighed. "I'm so sorry you had to learn the truth this way, honeybun."

"How could I have forgotten something so important?" She shook her head. "How did I so completely block my memories of that day at the cemetery?"

Unable to fully comprehend her mother's death,

had this been how her childish mind coped with unexplainable loss?

Deirdre hugged her. "It's going to be all right. You're not alone. You're no longer that lost little girl."

"How could I have been so blind?" Her eyelids stung. "It was Victoria who came for me. Victoria who loved me. Who held me when I cried for my mother."

Victoria who'd always been there for her. Despite AnnaBeth's determined efforts to push her away.

"All these years," AnnaBeth choked, "I blamed her for the distance in my relationship with my father, but it was my dad who never wanted a relationship with me in the first place."

Taking the blame, Victoria had covered for him so AnnaBeth wouldn't be hurt.

"I need to call her," she whispered. "Ask her to forgive me for how I treated her. Ask God to forgive me, too."

"You'll need time to come to terms with what you've discovered." Deirdre smoothed AnnaBeth's hair out of her face. "But there's no better place to find comfort than at the feet of the One who loves you so much." She glanced across the kitchen at her son. "Jonas?"

AnnaBeth lifted her gaze. He'd gone still, his face unreadable. She became aware, unlike his mother, he'd made no attempt to come to her. To soothe the blow she'd received.

Then what she'd said on the phone to her father registered. What Jonas had overheard. That it was AnnaBeth who walked out on Scott. Not the other way around.

Pushing back the chair, she shot to her feet. "Jonas."

But his dark eyes had grown opaque. Anger licked the broad outline of his face.

Deirdre's brow furrowed. "What's going on?" She glanced from her son to AnnaBeth. "What is it?"

"Mom, I think it would be best if you picked up Hunter from school today." Jonas's mouth flattened. "AnnaBeth and I need to talk. Now."

And she realized she'd made a terrible—perhaps unforgivable—mistake in not telling him the truth when she had the chance.

Chapter Fourteen

Lips pressed tightly together, Jonas's mother threw AnnaBeth a troubled glance, but left the lodge to retrieve Hunter from school. The door clicked shut behind her.

Jonas raised his chin. "You lied to me, Anna-Beth."

"No." She took a step across the kitchen toward him. "Not really."

"Your fiancé didn't jilt you at the altar. *You* jilted *him*."

Reddening, she tucked her hair behind her ear. "It was more complicated than that."

"What's so hard to understand? You ran away from him." Jonas glared at her. "But that's what you do, isn't it?" Hurt and anger simmered in his dark eyes. "When life gets tough, you run. How soon, I wonder, before you'd have turned tail on us?"

She threw out her hands. "It wasn't like that. If you'd only let me explain."

"I think we've both said about everything that needs to be said." His mouth flattened. "This only proves what a chump I was to ever believe anything that came out of your mouth."

She reached for him. "That's not true."

He shook off her hand. "We're from different worlds. We've been fooling ourselves."

She crossed her arms over her vest. "I don't believe that. You can't believe that, either. What we've felt... It was real. Every bit of it."

His lip curled. "What I believe is that you're just like Kasey."

She reared back. "Don't say that. You don't mean that."

"This holiday ranch vacation you've been on is nothing but a short break from reality." He grimaced. "For both of us."

How could she make him understand how she truly felt about him?

Jonas widened his stance, his boots a hip's width apart. "You and I would never work. Different worlds. Different dreams. Different goals."

"Please, Jonas..." How could she convince him they belonged together? "I should've told you about what happened from the beginning. I'm sorry. So sorry."

Everything she'd ever wanted was slipping

through her fingers. Suffocating fear almost consumed her. She wasn't too proud to beg him, to plead with him not to shut her out of his life. Because life without Jonas and Hunter meant not living at all.

And if she'd learned anything from her holiday sojourn in Truelove, it was that she had to fight for the love she wanted most.

"Jonas, if you could find it in your heart… Give me one more chance to show you—" The words she'd longed to say but feared to give voice to bubbled out. "I love you, Jonas. And I love Hunter so much."

She would do anything, sacrifice anything, if it meant they could have a future together.

"You don't know the meaning of the word *love*. You were supposed to love the man you left humiliated in Charlotte." He sneered. "Or is crushing hearts something you do for fun?"

"It wasn't like that." She wrung her hands. "Please let me explain…"

His face hardened. "I think you need to leave. Now."

The look in his eyes…

She sucked in a breath. "Jonas…"

But he'd stopped listening to her. Worse, he'd stopped *believing* in her.

Defaulting to self-protective mode, he turned

away. "You need to be gone before Hunter gets back from town with Mom."

How had everything gotten so out of control? She could see how he'd feel blindsided and betrayed, but this?

"B-but…" She couldn't seem to stop shaking. She clenched and unclenched her fists. "Hunter won't understand if I leave without saying goodbye."

His gaze raked her. "It's what people do. They leave." A muscle beat in his jaw. "Like the rest of us, he'll get used to it. We'll forget we ever met you."

Chest heaving, she stared at him. "Because I'm so forgettable?"

He flushed. "I didn't mean that the way it came out."

But she was so sick of emotionally unavailable men. And for the first time in her life, she made no attempt to stem her anger.

"Is it me you're really angry at for not pursuing a marriage I never truly wanted, Jonas, or yourself for not fighting for yours?"

He blanched. "Don't make this about me, AnnaBeth. I never lied to you."

"Maybe not." Her mouth twisted. "You just lie to yourself."

"Go, AnnaBeth." Sticking his hands in his pockets, he dropped his gaze. "Just go," he groaned.

Too overwhelmed for tears, she headed upstairs. It didn't take long to pack her scant belongings. Slinging the strap of her camera bag over her shoulder, she took one quick look around the bedroom.

But the only piece of herself she'd leave behind was her heart.

She slowly descended the stairs. Stalling? Praying for God to change his heart toward her.

AnnaBeth found him outside, restlessly pacing on the porch. As if he couldn't wait to be rid of her.

Her lips quivered, but before she could leave, Deirdre drove up with Hunter, who was peering out the window. Deirdre shut off the engine and got out of the Subaru.

"What's going on?" She cut her eyes to the suitcase in AnnaBeth's hand. "Jonas? AnnaBeth?"

Her emotions on autopilot, she deposited the bags in her car.

"AnnaBef!" Hunter raced up the sidewalk. "Where awe you going?"

Jonas grabbed hold of Hunter before he could reach AnnaBeth.

"Dad? Where's AnnaBef going? Dad!"

"I'm sorry…" she whispered to Deirdre. "You are all so dear to me."

"Dad!" Hunter wailed. "Don't let her go. Make her stay."

Holding him in place, Jonas clamped his hand

on Hunter's shoulder. "It's time for AnnaBeth to return to her real family, son. She doesn't belong here."

AnnaBeth wrenched open the car door.

"No…" Hunter's arms flailed, stretching toward her. "AnnaBef, don't weave me!"

AnnaBeth threw herself behind the wheel and shut herself inside.

She'd never wanted to leave them. But she had no one to blame but herself. If only she'd told Jonas from the beginning what happened the day of the wedding.

But she hadn't because she'd felt so unworthy. She'd been afraid Jonas would see her as unlovable, as she once believed herself. Now he felt lied to and deceived.

The look on his face was so fierce, so angry. So final in his unforgiveness.

She started the car and pulled away from the lodge. Her eyes darted to the rearview mirror.

"Come back, AnnaBef. Come back!" Hunter broke free from his father. "Don't weave me, AnnaBef," he shouted, running after her car. "I wuv you. I wuv you."

Then the car rumbled over the incline, and Hunter was lost from her view. Her heart shattered into a million crystals.

Reaching Interstate 40, without conscious thought, she headed southeast. Toward Charlotte.

It had been only ten days since she first traveled this road. Yet it felt she'd lived a lifetime since embarking on this journey. Everything she believed she knew about herself, life and God had been upended.

She'd met a man and his son. Found new friends, young and old, in a little mountain town called Truelove. Uncovered disturbing things about her past.

But somehow she'd discovered a peace and self-acceptance she'd never known before. And she'd finally understood her own worth in God's eyes.

It was a long way to Charlotte. She didn't cry. She'd moved beyond tears. Yet with every mile, the tension inside her chest wound tighter. The need for release became greater.

At long last, she pulled onto the exit ramp for Charlotte. Minutes later, she wheeled into the gated community she'd called home since she'd come to live with her father. The sun had already begun its slow descent behind the trees.

She whipped into the long driveway beside the stately, white Colonial, and flung herself out of the car. Tripping in her haste, she ran across the lawn. With only one thought in mind... With only one goal.

Clambering up the steps she burst through the front door. MaryDru's eyes went wide as she descended the staircase. "AnnaBeth?"

Her sister reached for her, but AnnaBeth swept past her and headed to the sunroom at the back of the house.

"AnnaBeth?" Letting the magazine drop from her hand, Victoria unfolded from the plump cushions of the sofa. "Is that you?"

Her red-rimmed, dark eyes sharpened behind the black framed eyeglasses. "Bethy? What's wrong? What's happened?"

Like a levee unable to hold back floodwater, she felt herself coming apart. Unraveling. Undone, she could barely see for the tears cascading down her cheeks.

She stumbled forward. "Mmm-Mom…"

And her mother opened her arms.

A few days later, Jonas sat alone in his truck on the frosty December morning. Engine idling to warm the vehicle before his son joined him, he stared unseeing at the ranch.

The final vestiges of snow had melted. Gone with AnnaBeth. The trees on the ridge lifted barren branches to the Carolina blue sky. As barren as his heart felt.

Jonas had tried stoking his anger against her, but even the anger deserted him, seeping away little more than twenty-four hours after her departure.

His mother jerked open the cab door, yanking

him from his bleak thoughts. Cold air poured into the truck. Clutching a small gift wrapped in gold foil, Hunter scrambled into his booster seat.

"Is that your Christmas present for your teacher, Hunt?"

Today was the preschool Christmas party. The one Jonas and AnnaBeth had planned to attend together.

Setting aside the gift, Hunter kept his head low, getting the buckle snapped. "Yes, sir."

Jonas chewed his lip.

Since AnnaBeth left, his son had been inconsolable. Holding his father responsible, he was angry with Jonas.

Lips pressed tight, his mother caught Jonas's gaze. Her disappointment in him was all too obvious.

She lifted her chin. "Could we meet for coffee at the Mason Jar about nine thirty?"

"I'm meeting Ethan at the Jar, anyway. I need an estimate on new rocking chairs for the cabins." He attempted a smile. "Coffee with my mom sounds like a great idea."

She didn't smile back. "You and I need to talk." His mother closed the truck door with a soft click.

His stomach cramped. Sounded like something he'd say to Hunter. When Hunter was in big trouble.

Trees flashing by on either side, the trip into

town felt long, and the silence between Jonas and his son, unbroken.

Jonas wasn't sure how to overcome the rift between him and this precious child for whom he would have gladly sacrificed his life. Instead of talking to his father, however, Hunter kept his feelings locked tight inside his little chest.

He flinched. A future Jonas in the making. And that, as much as anything, scared him to death.

At the preschool, he walked Hunter inside the building. But Hunter sprinted ahead as if he couldn't wait to be rid of him. He ducked his head inside the classroom to make sure his son was okay. And then headed out again. He met Callie and Jake coming in to drop off Maisie.

Callie glowered at him. "What were you thinking? To let that girl get away from you?" She threw out her hands. "Obviously, I gave you more credit for good sense than you deserve."

A plea for rescue, his gaze darted to Jake.

But looking sheepish, his friend shrugged. "Why don't I take Maisie to her class so she's not late for the party?"

Jonas swallowed. No reinforcements coming from that quarter. Mumbling something about an appointment, he made his escape to the parking lot.

He pulled the truck into the last available spot in front of the Jar. As usual, the diner was jam-packed.

When he stepped inside, heads swiveled at the sound of the jangling bell. And conversation immediately ground to a halt. From across the room Mayor Watson glared at him.

Among the breakfast crowd, he recognized people he'd known his entire life. Farmers like Callie's father, Nash Jackson. Local businessmen like his cousin, Zach, and fellow churchgoers.

Not one of them spared him a friendly glance. And when conversations resumed, he detected undercurrents of rumbling hostility. His face heated.

Ethan waved him over. At least he still had one friend.

Grateful, he stuffed his hands in his pockets and shuffled over. He rounded the corner of the booth to find Ethan's wife, Amber, on the other side. Incensed.

She scooted off the seat. "Are you an idiot?" she growled.

Apparently, he was.

"Just look what you've done to the matchmakers." She gestured toward the three ladies, slumped in the chairs at their table.

Amber slugged him in the arm. "How could you?"

"Ow!" Future stepsister or not, he thrust out his jaw. "I don't know what you think I've done to them, but I—"

"You've completely demoralized them is what you've done."

He flicked his eyes at Ethan. "What's she talking about?"

"Sorry, man." Ethan winced. "When Amber heard we were getting coffee..." Gaze lowering, he raised the mug to his lips.

"This is what I'm talking about, Jonas. Callie and Jake. Lorena and Nash." Amber ticked off the names on her fingers. "Me and Ethan. Your mom and my dad. And that's just counting the last twelve months."

He gulped.

"A perfect matchmaking record you've single-handedly managed to destroy."

His gaze strayed to the three matchmakers. Coffee untouched and cooling, ErmaJean, GeorgeAnne and IdaLee sat in stunned silence.

The bell jingled as his mom entered the diner.

"I'm sorry," he muttered.

"Don't be sorry," Amber hissed. "Fix it."

When Jonas's mother approached, Ethan slid out of the booth. "Give me a call later, okay?" He touched his wife's sleeve. "Come on, babycakes. It's his mom's turn at bat."

Great... He clamped his jaw. *Just great.*

The whole town was mad at him. AnnaBeth Cummings—Truelove's Sweetheart.

He plonked down in the vacated seat and laid

his hat beside him. "Why here, Mom? Why so public? You could've blasted me at home. Or is that the point?"

His mother sank across from him. "Not to humiliate you. But I knew if we talked here it would be easier for both of us to keep it together."

Letting his head fall backward, he exhaled. "Let me have it."

"Did you ask AnnaBeth why she ran away from Scott on her wedding day? Before your own baggage reared its ugly head?"

He straightened. "My what?"

She met his gaze head-on. "I'm talking about jumping to conclusions not based in fact. Because of what happened between you and Kasey. Because of the number that woman did on your head."

"I got over what happened with Kasey a long time ago, Mom," he grunted.

"Did you?" His mother placed her palms flat upon the table. "There are some wounds that can take a lifetime to heal."

He frowned.

"You're not the only one with abandonment issues. After what her father told her—" Tears sprang into his mother's eyes. "She was reeling, Jonas. And when you misunderstood…"

Had he somehow misunderstood? For the first time since that horrible morning, doubts emerged.

Jonas rested his palms on the sticky tabletop. "So tell me, Mom. Tell me what it is you think I should know."

"She and Scott weren't marrying for the right reasons, Jonas. AnnaBeth never loved him."

"Doesn't that tell you something about her, Mom?" He shook his head. "What kind of person in this day and age marries somebody they don't love?"

"What kind of person?" His mother pursed her lips. "Was love the reason you married Kasey?"

His overwhelming feeling for Kasey had consisted of guilt, not love. They'd been together only out of obligation to their unborn child.

"Like all of us, AnnaBeth has her own baggage." His mother opened her hands. "A desperate need for approval. That's why she agreed to marry Scott. To please her father."

He scrubbed his chin. "Always trying to live up to the impossibly perfect good-daughter image."

Like AnnaBeth and Kasey had told him, Jonas acknowledged it was his own baggage—pride and fear—that kept him emotionally unavailable. Closed off from love.

"When Victoria Cummings came to the ranch, she shared things with me about their family. About AnnaBeth…" His mother stared out the plate glass window overlooking Main. "About the family's code of silence."

The knot in his chest grew to fist-size proportions. "Code of silence? What are you talking about?"

"Victoria told me heartbreaking things about her own need to please. The life-long, self-defeating battle she'd waged for physical perfection." His mother took a deep breath. "About her husband's poverty-stricken childhood. Baggage that made him always striving to better himself. Never content. Demanding those around him do the same." His mother held Jonas's gaze. "Hayes Cummings is a functioning alcoholic, Jonas."

It made him sick to think about AnnaBeth growing up in such a self-destructive home. He closed his eyes.

"Life with her father meant constantly walking on eggshells." His mother bit her lip. "Her younger sister, MaryDru, struggles with anxiety issues. Everyone develops their own method of coping."

And for better or worse, AnnaBeth had developed hers—people-pleasing—no matter the personal cost.

"She's very protective of her sister. And loyal."

He looked up.

"Minutes before the wedding, AnnaBeth accidentally discovered MaryDru and Scott had fallen in love. Scott had decided to call off the wedding." His mother's lips thinned. "*He* was moments away from jilting AnnaBeth. She didn't lie to us, son."

"What happened?" he rasped.

"They didn't see AnnaBeth, but she overheard her sister insisting Scott follow through with the marriage." His mother's eyes misted. "MaryDru didn't want to see AnnaBeth get hurt."

"But she didn't know AnnaBeth didn't love Scott." Jonas gripped the edge of the table. "So instead of allowing MaryDru to make such a sacrifice—"

"AnnaBeth made the sacrifice for them. She was willing to take the blame. Accept the humiliation."

His temples pounded. "She ran because she knew if she stayed, somehow she'd be pressured into marrying Scott and breaking her sister's heart."

"Loyalty and love." His mother gave him a sad smile. "Hers is such a mixed-up family. And her world comes with such crushing societal expectations, too. Victoria asked me to pray for them."

"AnnaBeth tried to explain." He squeezed his eyes shut. "But I was horrible to her. I wouldn't listen. I said such terrible things to her. She must hate me."

"I don't think hatred is the primary feeling AnnaBeth Cummings has for you, my son. Question is, now that you know the truth, what do you intend to do about it?"

He opened his eyes. "I blew it, Mom. Just like I wrecked everything with Kasey."

A flood of emotion washed over him. And he knew if he didn't get out of the Jar this instant, he was going to lose it in front of the whole town.

He scrambled out of the booth.

She caught hold of his coat. "Jonas?"

"I—I need to go, Mom. Everything's my fault." He scrubbed his face with his hand. "But it's too late. It's too late."

Over the next few days, he walked around the ranch in a stupor. Wrestling with his own unresolved issues with his late wife. Until finally, humbled and spent, he gave them over to God. For the first time in four years, he felt the load of bitterness lift off his shoulders.

Now he only had to learn how to live with the heartache of a life without AnnaBeth. And somehow make amends for the hurt he'd inflicted in the heart of his child.

But living without AnnaBeth was easier said than done. The next few weeks were excruciating.

Without Jonas realizing it, like honeysuckle tendrils of AnnaBeth had found their way into every inch of his heart. And were about as easily eradicated.

He ought to know, 'cause he tried. But no mat

ter where he turned on the ranch, memories of her bombarded him.

Feeding the horses. Mucking out the barn. He thought of her in the hushed, almost holy stillness of the early morning mist on the mountain horizon. In the bright flash of a cardinal, red against a dark, evergreen bough.

And the ache in his heart only grew larger because she wasn't there to share those simple, everyday, exquisite joys with him.

He didn't laugh. He didn't smile. Each day seemed more dreary than the last. The final week before Christmas, he merely existed, and none too happily.

The loss of her was overwhelming. All-consuming. He could barely eat. Barely function. Sleep wasn't an option.

Christmas Eve morning found him making repairs to the roof of one of the cabins. He'd secured the last shingle when he spotted a messenger delivery vehicle pulling up to the lodge.

Pushing the brim of his hat higher on his forehead, he gazed without interest as his mother answered the door.

Not that it mattered. Not that anything mattered. How was it possible to fall so completely in love with someone in such a short course of time?

Truth be told—and it shocked him to his core—he'd lost his sense of place in the world. Lost his passion for the FieldStone at the same time he'd lost AnnaBeth. A revelation he'd never seen coming.

By the time he climbed off the roof and headed to the lodge, the vehicle was driving away.

His mother met him on the porch. "This came addressed to you." She handed him an expensive, ivory parchment envelope. "Special delivery."

He removed his work gloves and stuffed them in his pocket. "Who's it from?"

"The return address says Charlotte."

"Charlotte?" His heart pinched. "What is it?"

His mother tapped her shoe on the porch. "Open it and find out."

Mouth going dry, his hand shook as he slit the envelope open with the edge of his truck key. "It's an invitation."

Reading it, he forgot to breathe.

His mother touched his shoulder. "What is it, honey?"

"It—it's a w-wedding invitation." His voice cracked. "See for yourself."

His mother scanned the stationary. "'Mr. and Mrs. Hayes Cummings request the honor of your presence at the Christmas Eve wedding of their daughter at their home in Charlotte—'" She gasped. "That's tonight, Jonas."

"They got to her," he rasped.

He didn't know with whom he was more angry—AnnaBeth for giving in to the pressure for her father's approval? Or himself for not telling her how he felt when he had the chance?

God sending AnnaBeth to him had been a gift. And what had he done? Like an ungrateful child, he'd thrown the gift back in His face.

He lifted his hat and resettled it on his head. He'd made a terrible, perhaps irrevocable, mistake.

"I had it all wrong," he whispered.

On the surface, he and AnnaBeth were complete opposites. The rich city girl from the flatlands and the country-boy rancher from the mountains.

"We were perfect together."

His mother shook her head. "Perfection is an illusion, son. A mirage. Marriage is work, but with God at the center I recommend it highly."

Whereas he was more down-to-earth, AnnaBeth floated breezily through life like a balloon in a blue summer sky. But what they shared in common was more than enough for a happy life—their mutual love for Hunter, home, family and God.

Jonas kept AnnaBeth grounded. She'd taught him to not be afraid to dream. A wonderful recipe for happily-ever-after.

His mother squeezed his hand. "She's marrying someone else tonight."

Jonas rubbed his neck. "Where's Hunter, Mom?"

"At the twins' Christmas-Eve party 'til after lunch."

He glanced at his watch. "Tell him I had to take care of something for Christmas, but I'll be here to open presents tomorrow morning." He fisted his key.

"What do you intend to do, Jonas?"

"I'm running away to Charlotte." He squared his jaw. "And please pray that I don't come home empty-handed."

Chapter Fifteen

It was dark by the time he reached the city limits of Charlotte. After driving past the third extremely large house, he rechecked the coordinates to make sure he hadn't typed the wrong address into his phone's GPS. But there was no mistake.

His gut tightened. Block after block of exquisitely maintained lawns and estate-size homes. This was where AnnaBeth grew up. And he'd had her mucking out stalls.

The sports car clued him in that she'd come from wealthy people, but he'd never imagined this… His palms grew slick on the steering wheel. She always seemed so willing to lend a hand, no matter how menial the task. So he stopped thinking of her as a rich, flatlander debutante.

He pulled alongside the curb, letting the truck idle. He blew out a breath. Of course, she would live in the biggest of the big houses in this exclusive enclave. And the house was lit up like a Christmas tree. Parked cars clogged the street.

Jonas strangled the wheel. What was he doing? How could he even imagine a girl who grew up in this mansion would ever settle for an isolated, backwater ranch, or an unsophisticated guy like him? If he had any sense, he'd turn the truck around right now and hightail it back to the hills before he further humiliated himself.

But… His heart pounded as he gazed across the broad sweep of lawn… He didn't. He couldn't.

He turned off the ignition and got out of the vehicle. He'd come too far to turn back now. He wasn't leaving until he told AnnaBeth how he felt about her.

Taking long strides up the driveway, he called himself all kinds of a fool. He'd been wrong about so much. AnnaBeth did belong in his world. It was him who didn't belong in hers.

He readied himself to be thrown out on his ear by her very important father. After the way he'd treated their daughter, her family would probably hate him. But he couldn't rest—wouldn't rest—until he'd done everything in his power to prevent her from being bullied into marrying someone she didn't love.

If he'd given her half a chance in Truelove, she would've never come back here to marry tha Scott person. No matter if Jonas had blown hi chance with her, he couldn't stand by and watch her make a mistake that would ruin her life.

And if after he'd said what he should've said weeks ago she showed him the door, he'd go without protest. He'd be heartbroken. It didn't bear thinking about how devastated his son would be. But at least he'd know he'd done everything in his power to change her mind.

Music drifted from the house. There appeared to be a lot of people milling around inside. Taking a breath for courage, he climbed the steps. It was now or never. He was reaching for the brass handle when the door flew open, and an elegantly clad arm yanked him inside.

"About time." Diamond studs in her ears, Victoria shoved him forward. "I thought you'd never get here."

"What—?"

She disappeared into the throng, leaving him standing hat in hand in the foyer. Frowning at the partygoers, he got a bad feeling… It didn't so much look like a wedding about to commence as a wedding reception already in full swing.

Yet the invitation… He'd driven hard and fast. He ought to have been at least an hour ahead of the nuptials.

Maybe this was some prewedding shindig. Flatlanders. They did such strange, inexplicable things.

Just then, across the foyer, he caught a glimpse of a frothy concoction of lace and sequins. The bride. His heart raced at the prospect of seeing AnnaBeth again.

He started forward, but a thirtysomething man in a tux took AnnaBeth in his arms. Fists clenching, Jonas shouldered through the crowded entryway, trying to reach AnnaBeth.

"Give your new missus a kiss, Scott!" someone shouted.

Jonas stuttered to a stop at the base of the curving staircase.

Scott grinned. "My pleasure." Leaning over his bride, he took her face in his hands. "A kiss for Mrs. Scott Sullivan." Their lips met, and the house rang with cheers.

Pain rippled through Jonas. Knees suddenly weak, he staggered and fell into the newel post. A roaring filled his ears. His vision swam.

No... Please, no. This couldn't be happening.

"Jonas?"

But he was too late. He'd lost her. She was married. *Oh, God, help me. How am I ever going to live without her?*

"Jonas?"

Slowly, he became aware someone was calling his name and he returned to himself. Back to his unalterable, agonizing reality. He lifted his head. One hand gripping the banister, AnnaBeth peered at him from the landing. "What are you doing here?"

For one uncomprehending moment, he stared at her.

"Jonas?" Her lovely red hair was pulled into a knot at the nape of her neck. Much like the night they'd met.

He cut his gaze toward the jubilant scene across the foyer. The bride in her husband's arms. And to AnnaBeth standing a few steps above him. Her lacy green cocktail dress was lovely.

But it was not a wedding dress.

The air went out of him in a whoosh, and he sat down hard on the step.

She put her hand to the pearls at her throat. "Has something happened?"

There was no ring on her finger. He felt dizzy with relief.

"Is it Hunter?" Her voice hitched. She rushed down the steps, bridging the distance between them. "Is Hunter okay?" Sinking down beside him, she clutched Jonas's arm.

She wasn't married. Not yet. He wasn't too late. *Thank You, God.* He still had a chance. He must—

AnnaBeth shook him. "Jonas!"

Fear, anger and something else warred in her beautiful, emerald eyes. Her hand tightened on his arm.

"Hunt's okay." He swallowed. "Other than crying himself to sleep every night since you left."

Tears filled her eyes. "Oh." She turned her face toward the wall.

His heart hammered. He didn't like not being able to see her face. She had the most expressive face. What must it be like to wear your feelings so transparently for everyone to see?

Once upon a time, he'd believed hope lost. But then he'd met her. She held his entire future in her hands. Every hope, he'd only just begun to dream.

He blew out a breath. "You're not married, right?"

She turned to him. "What?"

"You haven't married Scott yet, have you, AnnaBeth?"

She blinked. "Of course I haven't married Scott." She pressed her lips together. "Why are you here, Jonas? Why did you come?"

He'd hurt her, badly. But if she gave him the chance, he'd gladly spend the rest of his life doing his best to ensure nothing ever hurt her again.

"I came to stop you from marrying Scott tonight."

She frowned. "Why on earth would you think I was marrying Scott?"

He lifted his chin. "The wedding invitation…"

Letting his hat roll onto the hardwood floor, he

dug the crumpled invitation from his coat pocket and handed it to AnnaBeth.

She read the invitation aloud. "'Mr. and Mrs. Hayes Cummings request the honor of your presence at the Christmas Eve wedding of their daughter ...'" She looked up from the paper.

Their eyes locked.

His Adam's apple bobbed. "But it didn't specify which daughter." He closed his eyes. "MaryDru," he rasped. "MaryDru and Scott were married tonight. Not you."

"You thought I was marrying Scott."

His eyes snapped open and fastened on her face.

"That doesn't explain why you drove all this way."

"I thought your family had pressured you into getting married." He scraped his hand over his face. "Hunter isn't the only one who missed you, AnnaBeth."

Dropping her gaze, she smoothed her skirt over her knees. "I've missed the FieldStone. Deirdre. The matchmakers. Truelove."

He took hold of her hand. "But not me?"

Like a startled bird, her eyelashes flew upward. "Oh, Jonas," she whispered. "You, most of all."

It had to mean something that he'd traveled so far to see her tonight. He must care for her, if only a little, if he'd come to prevent her from making a mistake.

AnnaBeth took a deep breath. "Since I came home, things have been different. Daddy got out of detox. He's been sober for nearly three weeks. He and Mom are seeing a marriage counselor, too. I have real hope they'll stay together."

Jonas cocked his head. "Mom?"

"Victoria is the true heart of my family." Anna-Beth smiled. "She's always loved me. Loved all of us, even when we were so very unloving. We've all grown closer. Daddy, Mom, MaryDru and me."

"Please forgive me, AnnaBeth, for the things I said to you. You're nothing like Kasey. But I was afraid..."

He paused for a moment, taking a deep breath.

"I've been afraid of so much. Of getting hurt again. Of not being enough. But more than anything else, I've been afraid that you didn't love me anymore."

She shook her head. "I love you, Jonas. And whether you loved me or not, that was never going to change. Love doesn't work that way."

Touching his lips to her hand, he gazed deep into her eyes.

"I love you, AnnaBeth Cummings. Forgive me for sending you away. I was an idiot. I've been lost without you. I'm nothing without you."

"Jonas..."

"I love you for your sweetness. For your kindness. I love the brightness you bring into my life." His gaze raked her face. "I love your hair. I love every single bit of you. I love the way you love my son."

"Oh, Jonas…if you make my mascara run, Mom's going to have a fit."

Cradling her face in his palm, he swiped the pad of his thumb across the apple of her cheek. "Marry me, AnnaBeth. Please. I want to spend the rest of my life loving you. Loving our son."

"Our son?"

He nodded. "Because somehow, I think Hunter's always been yours. Just like me, he's been waiting his whole life to find you. Waiting for you to run away in a blinding snowstorm and find us."

Thank You, God. Thank You for bringing this cowboy, his son and this love into my life.

"It was never me rescuing you." He kissed the lone tear away with his lips. "It was always you rescuing me from myself."

Brushing his lips across her mouth, he rested his forehead against hers. "Will you marry me, AnnaBeth? Because my heart has finally found its true home. With you." He exhaled. "Though I realize I have so little to offer you—"

"You give me everything I'll ever need when you give me yourself, Jonas Stone." She locked her hands at the nape of his neck. "All I ever wanted."

"But you've got a whole other life here. A life I know nothing about. But I'd like to learn." His gaze bored into hers. "Maybe your mom could recommend a neighborhood I could afford with good schools for Hunter."

"You'd move to here, to Charlotte? What about the FieldStone? Ranching is in your blood. The mountains are the oxygen in your lungs."

He gave her that ridiculously stomach-quivering smile that made her glad she was already sitting down.

"You, AnnaBeth Cummings, are in my blood. You are the oxygen in my lungs. You are the only thing besides my son I can't face life without."

"But—"

"No buts." He squeezed her hands. "Your dreams are important. Important to both me and Hunter."

Her heart felt so full. Light and free. That he'd be willing to give up his heritage, to move away from everyone and everything he'd ever known. For her…

Jonas's smile fell a notch. "You haven't said… If you'll mar—"

"Of course I'll marry you." She threw her arms around him again. "Yes. Yes. Yes."

His kiss was everything she'd dreamed this moment would be. Achingly sweet. With a protective tenderness that robbed her of breath.

"I love you, AnnaBeth. So much. And I want to do this the right way." Rising, he offered his hand to her. "I want to meet your family."

Suddenly, Victoria joined them. "Hayes is anxious to meet you, too, Jonas."

AnnaBeth smoothed out the invitation. "This was your doing, wasn't it, Mom? You sent Jonas the altered invitation."

She touched AnnaBeth's face. "Happy, my darlin' girl?"

Giving her a tremulous smile, AnnaBeth nodded. "I am. Very."

"Just as I prayed." Victoria winked at Jonas. "And it wasn't only me. MaryDru was also in on the matchmaking to bring you two together."

She gave a thumbs-up to MaryDru standing across the foyer with her new husband's arm around her tiny waist. Bouquet in hand, Mary-Dru did a fist pump.

Victoria whipped out her phone and began to type.

"Who are you texting, Mom?"

"The Truelove Matchmakers."

AnnaBeth and Jonas exchanged glances. "Seriously?"

"MaryDru and I had a conference call with them earlier this week." Victoria hit Send. "They've made both of us honorary matchmakers. You didn't think I pulled off this first one by myself, did you?"

AnnaBeth's eyebrows rose. "First one?"

Batting her lashes, Victoria smiled. "I've decided to open a Charlotte branch of the Truelove Matchmakers club."

Jonas laughed.

AnnaBeth kissed her cheek. "The Queen City will never know what hit them."

Jonas laced his fingers into hers. "I need to talk to your father… Ask for his blessing."

She was so, so happy. She hadn't known she could feel this happy. She squeezed his hand. "Let's find Daddy. But then—" she gave him a wide smile "—I want to be at the FieldStone for Hunter when he wakes up on Christmas morning."

AnnaBeth's father not only gave Jonas his blessing, but he also insisted on announcing their engagement to the guests gathered for her sister's wedding reception.

Her father's once handsome face bore the signs of dissipation, but a serenity also rested on his features. A peace Jonas suspected had not always been there.

"AnnaBeth has been so heartbroken these last few weeks." The silver-haired patrician gripped Jonas's hand. "Too often, I've let her down." His gaze landed on Victoria. "I've let all my girls down, but I hope you'll love AnnaBeth the way she deserves to be loved."

MaryDru, AnnaBeth's sister, joined them with her groom. "Or you'll have to answer to me."

Victoria nudged him with her bony elbow. "And me."

But he had to love and respect someone who loved AnnaBeth as fiercely as Victoria Cummings. Because he felt the same. He loved AnnaBeth, too.

He was cautiously encouraged by the changes he saw in AnnaBeth's relationship with her father. With her entire family. But he knew these were wounds that might take a lifetime to fully heal.

Once AnnaBeth explained about Hunter's Christmas mommy wish, Victoria practically threw them out the door.

"I hope you'll share your little guy with us." A wistful expression crossed her lovely features. "AnnaBeth sure loves him."

Jonas nodded. "Hunter loves her right back."

Eyes brimming, AnnaBeth hugged Victoria. "I love you, Mom."

Victoria kissed her forehead. "Be happy, my darlin' Bethy." Rapidly blinking, she fanned her face. "Oh, no. My mascara!"

With tentative plans for a New Year's weekend at the ranch to bring both families together, he finally got AnnaBeth into the truck, with Victoria sending them off. As it turned out, Victoria also sent gifts to Hunter and Jonas's mother.

AnnaBeth rolled her eyes.

"What?" Victoria closed the cab door with a click. "I totally expected a happy ending. And you know how I love to shop."

One special present, however, AnnaBeth cradled carefully in her lap. It was a small, green velvet square box with an overlarge ivory silk bow. She'd put it together herself. Hunter's name was on the gift tag.

Pulling onto the interstate, Jonas flicked his eyes at her. "Is there any reason why you're sitting over there, and I'm way over here?"

Smiling, she slid over, nestling against his side. "I can't think of one good reason in the world."

The night sky had begun to lighten when he steered the truck through the stone gateposts of the FieldStone Ranch. Errant rays of light emerging beyond the ridge threw the mountains in silhouette, spearing the darkness.

She drew in a deep breath.

He cut his eyes at her. "Second thoughts?"

She touched her finger to the space between his brows. "Stop frowning." She smoothed the crease, a smile playing about her lips. "You're stuck with me now. No second thoughts, I'm just happy to be home."

"Home?" he rasped. "What about Charlotte?"

She rested her head against his shoulder. "There's nowhere I want to be but here, Jonas. This is where I belong. I can continue to write the blog from the FieldStone. It will be even better because *Heart's Home* will have finally found its truest home with you and Hunter."

A lump rose in his throat. "I never want the FieldStone to come between us the way it came between..." Emotion clogging his voice, he pulled to a stop in front of the darkened lodge.

Capturing his face between her palms, she pulled his face toward hers. "God has given us both a second chance at love. With His help, we'll make this work. No more running away. I'll never leave you, I promise."

He kissed her cheek.

The velvet box in her hands, she inched over to the cab door. "But now it's time to go see my boy."

Her boy... She not only already had Jonas's heart, but she also had Hunter's, too.

Looking over her shoulder at him, she smiled. "I have a certain Christmas wish to fulfill."

His heart swelled with more happiness than he'd ever believed it could hold.

Lips curving, he followed her into the house. In the living room, a small fire crackled in the fireplace. The massive tree twinkled with bright, colorful lights.

"Jonas?" His mother unfolded from the sofa.

"I didn't mean to fall asleep. Is that you, Anna-Beth?" Catching sight of his beautiful runaway bride, his mother's voice hitched. "Oh, honeybun. I'm so glad you're back."

Rushing forward, his mother embraced Anna-Beth. There was a lot of hugging and soft laughter. Tears, too.

Until a thump from upstairs.

He smiled. "Hunter's awake."

"Oh." AnnaBeth fluttered her hands. "Quick. Put the gift under the tree."

Boots clattered across the floorboards upstairs. Hunter's bedroom door creaked open.

"Here." Snatching a big purple bow off another present, his mother stuck its adhesive edge atop AnnaBeth's head. Just in time, she shuffled AnnaBeth out of sight.

Cowboy pajama pants tucked into his boots, Hunter clomped down the stairs.

"Merry Christmas, Hunter." Jonas hugged his son. "It's going to be the happiest Christmas ever," he whispered in Hunter's ear.

Frowning, Hunter rubbed the sleep from his eyes. "Where were you, Dad?"

"I told you he'd be back this morning." His mother beckoned his son. "Come see what Santa—" she winked at Jonas "—brought you this fine Christmas morn."

Hair mussed from sleep, Hunter crouched by

the green velvet box under the tree. "What's dis?" Brow creased, he looked from his grandmother to his father. "Where did dis come from?"

Jonas squatted beside him. "What does the tag say?"

"It says my name." His voice rose. "For Hunter. Wight, Dad?"

He grinned. "It sure does. It's a special gift. From someone who loves you very much."

"From you, Dad?"

He shook his head. "Nope. Though I do love you a lot."

"From you, Gwam-ma?"

"I love you, too, Hunter." His grandmother eased into the nearby armchair. "But it's not from me."

Hunter shrugged his pajama-clad flannel shoulders. "Den who?"

"Open it, Hunter." Jonas laughed. "Open it and see."

"It's weally pwetty."

Jonas smiled. "The outside is pretty, but I think you're going to love the inside even more."

Lifting off the velvet-wrapped lid, Hunter peered into the box. "It's a piece of paper."

His grandmother clapped her hands together. "Take it out. Let's read it."

Chewing his cheek, Hunter pulled out the page of ivory stationary. He held it out to his father.

By the light of the Christmas tree, Jonas ran his finger under each word. "For Hunter Stone— a Christmas mommy."

Hunter's eyes went large. "A Chwistmas mommy?" He scrambled to his feet. "Where?"

AnnaBeth popped out from behind the stairs. "Can I be your Christmas mommy, Hunter?"

With a small cry, he dashed across the living room. AnnaBeth opened her arms wide.

"You came back!" Arms encircling her legs, he buried his face into her waist. "I wuv you so much, AnnaBef. I wuv you so much."

Bending over him, her hands flew, stroking his hair, his face and back again. Tears flowing across her cheeks, she whispered sweet words of love into his son's ear.

His mom hugged Jonas. "They're so wonderful with each other," she whispered.

Thank You, God, for bringing us together.

His mother swiped her eyes. "I'm going to fix everyone the biggest breakfast ever." She slipped away toward the kitchen.

Jonas cleared his throat. "Is there r-room for one m-more?"

Lifting his son into her arms, AnnaBeth smiled. "There's always room for your dad, right Hunter?"

Hunter tucked his head into the hollow of he throat. "I wuv you, AnnaBef. I wuv you, Dad."

She kissed Hunter's hair. "Dad and I love you so much."

Hunter stuck his finger in the corner of his mouth. Something Jonas hadn't seen him do since he was a toddler.

"Is it okay to caw you Mommy or..." His little chin wobbled. "Awe you still AnnaBef?"

"I'm going to be your mommy, Hunter." Closing her eyes, her lips brushed his forehead. "Forever."

Jonas—who prided himself for always keeping his emotions in check—couldn't for the life of him seem to stop the flow of tears.

He swiped his cheeks. "I'm dying over here wanting a hug from you two."

"Dad needs us, Hunt." She smiled at Jonas. "Let's go take care of him."

Shifting Hunter onto her hip, she brought his son to the Christmas tree.

Keeping one arm firmly locked around his Christmas mommy, Hunter threw his other arm around Jonas, drawing the three of them into one unit. The family they were always meant to be.

Suddenly, Hunter lifted his head. "Dad! Mommy! Wook!" He pointed to the window. "It's snowing."

Like feathers from a quilt, large, delicate flakes floated from the sky.

AnnaBeth hugged them tight. "Another Christmas gift from our Father."

Hunter's eyes shone. "We got our snow pwincess, Dad."

And with everyone he loved safe within these walls, a lightness, unlike any he'd known since he was a boy, filled Jonas.

He kissed his son. Then kissed his beautiful, runaway snow bride.

"We sure did, Hunter. We sure did."

* * * * *

If you loved this book,
be sure to check out Lisa Carter's
other heartwarming stories

The Deputy's Perfect Match
The Bachelor's Unexpected Family
The Christmas Baby
Hometown Reunion
His Secret Daughter
The Twin Bargain

Find these and other great reads
at www.LoveInspired.com

Dear Reader,

Welcome to Truelove, North Carolina, set in the breathtakingly lovely Blue Ridge Mountains of North Carolina.

Though the course of true love doesn't always run smooth, never fear. The Truelove Matchmakers are there to make sure everyone finds their happily-ever-after.

The heart of this story is about a man searching for a love that will never leave or desert him. It's also about a woman searching for a place to belong. This story is about trusting God. With the good. With the bad. With everything.

As AnnaBeth discovers at the FieldStone Ranch, no matter how tragic the past, God has a place of belonging for each of us. And most importantly, she learns to see herself from God's perspective.

You, too, dear reader, are so beautiful to Him. A precious jewel. And so beloved.

This is why I wrote this story. And because it is my prayer that you will ultimately find in Him your home. The happily-ever-after for which you were truly made.

I hope you have enjoyed taking this journey with AnnaBeth, Hunter and Jonas. I would love to hear from you. You may email me at lisa@lisacarterauthor.com or visit www.lisacarterauthor.com.

In His Love,
Lisa Carter

Get 4 FREE REWARDS!

We'll send you 2 FREE Books <u>plus</u> 2 FREE Mystery Gifts.

HEARTWARMING

Safe in His Arms

Anna J. Stewart

HEARTWARMING

The Rancher's Family

Barbara White Daille

Harlequin® Heartwarming™ Larger-Print books feature traditional values of home, family, community and—most of all—love.

FREE Value Over $20

YES! Please send me 2 FREE Harlequin® Heartwarming™ Larger-Print novels and my 2 FREE mystery gifts (gifts worth about $10 retail). After receiving them, if I don't wish to receive any more books, I can return the shipping statement marked "cancel." If I don't cancel, I will receive 4 brand-new larger-print novels every month and be billed just $5.74 per book in the U.S. or $6.24 per book in Canada. That's a savings of at least 21% off the cover price. It's quite a bargain! Shipping and handling is just 50¢ per book in the U.S. and $1.25 per book in Canada.* I understand that accepting the 2 free books and gifts places me under no obligation to buy anything. I can always return a shipment and cancel at any time. The free books and gifts are mine to keep no matter what I decide.

161/361 HDN GNPZ

Name (please print)

Address   Apt. #

City   State/Province   Zip/Postal Code

Mail to the **Reader Service:**
IN U.S.A.: P.O. Box 1341, Buffalo, NY 14240-8531
IN CANADA: P.O. Box 603, Fort Erie, Ontario L2A 5X3

Want to try 2 free books from another series? Call 1-800-873-8635 or visit www.ReaderService.com.

---

*Terms and prices subject to change without notice. Prices do not include sales taxes, which will be charged (if applicable) based on your state or country of residence. Canadian residents will be charged applicable taxes. Offer not valid in Quebec. This offer is limited to one order per household. Books received may not be as shown. Not valid for current subscribers to Harlequin Heartwarming Larger-Print books. All orders subject to approval. Credit or debit balances in a customer's account(s) may be offset by any other outstanding balance owed by or to the customer. Please allow 4 to 6 weeks for delivery. Offer available while quantities last.

Your Privacy—The Reader Service is committed to protecting your privacy. Our Privacy Policy is available online at www.ReaderService.com or upon request from the Reader Service. We make a portion of our mailing list available to reputable third parties that offer products we believe may interest you. If you prefer that we not exchange your name with third parties, or if you wish to clarify or modify your communication preferences, please visit us at www.ReaderService.com/consumerschoice or write to us at Reader Service Preference Service, P.O. Box 9062, Buffalo, NY 14240-9062. Include your complete name and address.

HW20

THE FORTUNES OF TEXAS COLLECTION!

18 FREE BOOKS in all!

Treat yourself to the rich legacy of the Fortune and Mendoza clans in this remarkable 50-book collection. This collection is packed with cowboys, tycoons and Texas-sized romances!

YES! Please send me **The Fortunes of Texas Collection** in Larger Print. This collection begins with 3 FREE books and 2 FREE gifts in the first shipment. Along with my 3 free books, I'll also get the next 4 books from The Fortunes of Texas Collection, in LARGER PRINT, which I may either return and owe nothing, or keep for the low price of $5.24 U.S./$5.89 CDN each plus $2.99 for shipping and handling per shipment*. If I decide to continue, about once a month for 8 months I will get 6 or 7 more books but will only need to pay for 4. That means 2 or 3 books in every shipment will be FREE! If I decide to keep the entire collection, I'll have paid for only 32 books because 18 books are FREE! I understand that accepting the 3 free books and gifts places me under no obligation to buy anything. I can always return a shipment and cancel at any time. My free books and gifts are mine to keep no matter what I decide.

☐ 269 HCN 4622   ☐ 469 HCN 4622

Name (please print)

Address   Apt. #

City   State/Province   Zip/Postal Code

Mail to the **Reader Service:**
IN U.S.A.: P.O. Box 1341, Buffalo, N.Y. 14240-8531
IN CANADA: P.O. Box 603, Fort Erie, Ontario L2A 5X3

Love Inspired

A new mom for Christmas?
She's everything they've wished for.

Runaway bride AnnaBeth Cummings
needs shelter for the holidays when a
blizzard leaves her stranded, and rancher
Jonas Stone's happy to help. But his son's
been wishing for a mommy for Christmas, and
town matchmakers are convinced AnnaBeth
and Jonas are perfect for each other. As
the stor... ...ty girl AnnaBeth will
...oes her heart now
...g in the country?

$7.25 U.S./$8.25 CAN.

ISBN-13: 978-1-335-53962-5

50725

CATEGORY
INSPIRATIONAL

HARLEQUIN®
LOVE INSPIRED®

harlequin.com